GUNNAR KOPPERUD

LONGING

Translated from the Norwegian by Christopher Jamieson

BLOOMSBURY

First published in Great Britain in this revised edition 2002

First published in Norwegian
by J.M. Stenersens Forlag A/S 1999 under the title *Savn*

Copyright © Gunstein Kopperud 1999, 2002
English translation copyright © Christopher Jamieson 2002

ACKNOWLEDGEMENTS

The quotations from Isabelle Eberhardt on pp. 26–33 are based
on the translation by Paul Bowles, *The Oblivion Seekers and Other Writings*,
London: Peter Owen Ltd, 1988
Verses from the Koran on pp. 45, 48, 53, 54 are taken from
the translation by J. M. Rodwell, London: Dent, 1909, reissued 1992
The quotation from Don McCullin on pp. 208–9
is from *A Life in Photographs*, first published in *Granta* no. 14, 1984

The publishers gratefully acknowledge a grant
from NORLA towards the translation of this book

The moral right of the author has been asserted

Bloomsbury Publishing Plc, 38 Soho Square, London W1D 3HB

A CIP catalogue record for this book is available from the British Library

ISBN 0 7475 5343 2

10 9 8 7 6 5 4 3 2 1

Typeset by Hewer Text Composition Services, Edinburgh
Printed in Great Britain by Clays Ltd, St Ives plc

LONGING

A brown envelope floats on an endless blue sea. It can't have been there long, the name and address are still legible, written in black ink, and the stamps are still attached. Yet it seems as if it has always been there; it has the same timelessness about it as the horizon all around, the same air of abandonment.

Below the envelope a shimmer of white, sheets of paper slowly curling and twisting in the water, reflecting the sunlight. The motion of the sea gives life and form to the pages: varying shapes, now a face, a pair of eyes, a hand; now a ballet in white, a man gently lifting a woman, a horse galloping over a plain. The envelope is floating silently above the pages like a pensive, half-sleeping face; it makes them seem like dreams, swirling up or down in the depths.

The horizon is still and empty, infinity pierced at just one point by a black cliff towering up into the sky. It was not here that it started, but something started here: the face and the eyes and the hand started here. This was where he had come with her after she was demobilized and had handed in her weapons, after he had been told by his newspaper to take things easy for a while.

OBLIVION

I was with her the first time she went back to her village. We travelled by bus for two nights and a day; at night she sat with her head on my shoulder and her eyes closed, by day she had her forehead pressed to the window looking out. Neither of us said anything in particular. The other people on the bus cast covert glances at us and whispered to one another; a woman in front held out a bag of roasted nuts, a young boy in the seat behind proffered a bottle of water. She was still in uniform, and I could see it reflected as respect in the others' eyes. At night when she wrapped her dark burnous around her like a blanket they studied her more overtly. I made notes about the landscape as it slid past in constant variation, from barren high plains to fertile lowland, from broad daylight to camp fires and velvety soft night; I noted the smells on the bus, of chickens and pigs and sour milk and sweaty skin; I noted the sounds of the diesel engine and monotonous music, of laughter and scraps of conversation.

As the last veil of night dissolved behind us we arrived at the coast. We walked over cobbles down a narrow street from the bus station towards the harbour. At the quay lay the ferry that was to take us out to the island, the same ferry she had left by. She stood and stared when she caught sight of it. We found ourselves a place on the upper deck and settled down to wait in patience. The ferry had arrived that morning and would not be leaving until it was full; that was the custom. She slept a little and awoke to the throb of the engine. We stood together at the rail and watched the land dwindle and evaporate, colours and contours merging. We had something to eat and talked and read for a while, and sailed into the harbour of her island just as the sun was dipping into the ocean.

I wondered if there would be anyone there to meet her; they knew she was coming. I asked her what she thought, and she looked at me before correcting me.

'Us.'

The harbour was no more than a hundred metres wide, and fifty metres offshore a mole had been built with a storm light on it. From the street alongside the harbour small stone houses were stacked up the hillside towards the top of the island, red, blue, yellow, green; a dozen fishing boats in the same colours were drawn up on the beach. Shops and stalls lined the street by the harbour and there was an open square by the quay where the people waiting for the ferry had gathered. She was hailed by a youth, and then another, waving; she leaned over the rail and gave a little sob. Her eyes were scanning the island as if to make sure that everything was still present, and when she saw the two youths there was something akin to sorrow in her eyes. I understood why when she threw her arms round their necks: they were her brothers, small boys when she left, now young men. Catching one another's eye, they gave me a friendly greeting, then picked up our bags and carried them on their heads as they led the way up on to the island.

She chatted to them as we walked along, and they became increasingly confident, their tension melting away, able to breathe and shout and laugh again. One of them cautiously took hold of the sleeve of her uniform, the other walked backwards in front of her as he conversed, full of excitement and laughter. All around us people came out on to their verandahs to look at her, at us, mostly older women, and they clapped their hands and called to her. She raised her head and smiled, and in that smile I saw the rest of my life. A woman came out of a house and embraced her in tears, another threw flowers from a window; an old man shook my hand and thanked me, in Italian, and I thought, don't thank me, it wasn't me who won the war.

Her house was painted blue with white window frames and a white door, and running the length of the wall was a flowerbed edged with green bottle shards. There was an olive grove to one side with a view over the harbour and the sea. Her mother was waiting in the doorway, a strong, stately woman with large hands and penetrating eyes. She was darker skinned than her daughter, but had the same straight nose and high brow. She stepped forward as we came through the gate of the tiny front garden and stood hands on hips staring at her daughter. We stopped too, and mother and daughter just stared at each other for a long time in silence, almost threateningly, as if they were gauging each other's strength. Then the mother gave a cry, loud and angry, and the daughter replied, just as loud, just as angrily, before the mother had finished. The mother smacked her right fist into her left palm and gave another cry, the daughter stamped on the ground in fury and stabbed the air as she screamed a response. The two brothers retreated nervously. Then her mother ran the few steps over to us, seized her daughter's uniform at the waist with both hands and tugged at it as she uttered something that sounded like a question. Her daughter jerked her body as if to tear herself free, but her mother didn't let go, her hands moved from her daughter's waist to around her back, she turned her face up to her daughter's and her eyes filled with tears, and her daughter took her in her arms and let her head fall on her breast. A man appeared in the doorway, likewise strong and stately, in a white cotton jellaba, with a grey beard and two gold teeth. He came up to the daughter and spoke, and she turned her head from her weeping mother towards me.

'He offers you his apologies, he didn't know you were coming. He asks if he can invite you in for a glass of tea.'

'With pleasure.'

He smiled as she conveyed his message, stood aside and motioned towards the house with his hand. As I passed the two women, I saw the mother look quickly in my direction.

I knew my mother would be angry when she saw me; she always was when she had been worried about me. I had always answered back, never accepting a reprimand from anyone.

'So many years and not a single word!'

She was shouting, with her hands on her hips.

'You know perfectly well we weren't allowed to write!'

'What kind of daughter is it that leaves her mother and her brothers and sister to go off and live with strange men?'

She struck out with her hand to show what she meant.

'What are you implying?'

She ran over to me and grabbed at my uniform.

'And these clothes, are they clothes for a young woman?'

She met my eyes with hers, and I saw them fill with tears as she held me and I took her in my arms. Her husband, the same man as when I left, appeared in the doorway.

'Welcome home. I see you're not alone. Who is he?'

'A friend.'

'Please give him my apologies for not coming down to the harbour to welcome him. Will you invite him in for tea?'

I noticed mother looking hard at him as he went past.

He proved that he was no stranger to our customs with the same naturalness that had shown he was no stranger to life at the front. He put his left hand on his right lower arm when he shook hands, he removed his shoes at the door, he adopted the correct posture on the floor. It was like getting to know him all over again, or getting to know him through my mother, different sides of him; I could see that she was watching him, studying his behaviour. He tried to avoid her eyes, since she was another man's woman. When my little sister came round with the water bowl for us to wash our hands, he lowered his gaze; when he was served tea first, he drained the glass in two gulps and gave it back to my mother so that she could rinse it and give tea to the others. I saw her becoming more relaxed, feeling more secure; she didn't know much about white men, but she had heard that they were ill-mannered.

He asked my mother's husband about his family and listened respectfully, he spoke of his own family, going back thirteen generations, the way it should be done. He enquired about the country and the war and about those who had gone away; he spoke of his own country, and of the war there, a long time ago. As he talked he looked at me, and whenever I had to help him with a word he looked at my mother's husband. He didn't say anything after my mother's husband had left the room to slaughter a goat for us, as if he were leaving it to us to decide whether we wanted to converse with him or with one another.

My mother said in a low voice, 'You're looking him in the eyes.'

'That's what we did at the front.'

'You're not at the front now.'

She gave him another glass of tea, and he thanked her with a smile, but with a faraway expression: he had already left the room and was elsewhere – a trait in him that I found unsettling.

'What else did you do at the front?'

'Mother, I don't want any of that. If you go on like that I'll leave.'

'What sort of respect is that to show for your mother?'

'What sort of respect is it to think that of your daughter?'

'Does he share our faith?'

I knew the question would come, I had been dreading it. I knew that if I could get him to raise his right hand then and there and repeat after me, *la illaha illa Allah, Mohammed rassul Allah*, my mother would be convinced, because she would be incapable of imagining that anyone could say the words without meaning them, and I knew that he would never be accepted without being of our faith; but the years at the front had affected me, changed me, I felt pulled in two directions instead of just one.

'Not yet.'

Mother looked at me and suddenly I was a little girl again.

'Anyway, you're already promised.'

'What do you mean?'

I saw that he was watching me, that he realized I had been upset by something.

'Your stepfather's cousin.'

'The cigarette vendor?'

'He doesn't do that any more, he's a foreman in the olive grove now. A good man. Your horoscopes agree.'

'Why didn't you wait till I was back?'

'We needed the dowry to be able to afford to marry off your brothers.'

'Have you taken the dowry in advance?'

'The first instalment.'

'And paid in advance for those two?'

'The first instalment.'

I knew the next thing I said would determine my status in the household from then on, I knew I had to think before I answered. We had speculated about this in the Movement as we grew up into women, about how it would be when we came back to our villages one day and found that there time had stood still, and that our parents continued to regard us as children.

I heard him stir behind me and turned to look at him. There was something in his eyes, something he had understood.

'Can I take my friend to the bench in the olive grove and show him the view?'

'Of course. Your brother can go with you. We'll call you when the meal is ready.'

His hand brushed mine as we walked to the bench. I told him to sit down and I sat beside him. It was a clear evening with a velvet sky; everything on the island was very distinct, easy to point out. I showed him my childhood: there were the steps my father had made, there the school, there the market; I showed him my roots: there the mosque, there the meeting house for the Council of Elders, there the house where we held celebrations; I showed him the initial stages of my departure from the parental home: where I had my first meeting with the Movement, where I first pasted up illegal posters, where I first distributed illegal pamphlets. And I knew as I talked and pointed that there must be a place that had the same significance for him, everyone has such a place, and which is right, to leave it or to stay?

———

A ship sailed away from the island while she was talking and pointing things out to me. It was not the ferry, but a cargo boat in rusty blue and white with a tricolour flag at the stern and a pennant on the mast. It was low amidships as if for hauling in nets. I followed it with my eyes as she spoke: it chugged out of the little harbour, passed the mole with its storm light and set course towards the horizon. I turned my gaze through 180 degrees; the horizon was unbroken, with no sign of land. The cargo boat got smaller and smaller, the horizon bigger and bigger, and I tried to imagine how it might feel to be standing at the rudder and steering towards an empty horizon, leaving the island behind and heading for the space between sea and sky without knowing whether there was actually anything there.

Her voice was rather weak, as if something were pressing on it from within. I had a feeling I knew what it was, but didn't dare ask. I could see her quite clearly going to the Movement's meeting house for the first time. Had she become a teenager by then? It was hard to say, her face was almost that of an adult, her body still ungainly. I could see her pasting up posters with quick, gentle motions, I could see her distributing pamphlets to surprised adults and disappearing down an alley at the sound of a whistle.

I followed her eyes as she indicated the school, but it remained closed for me, a yellow building surrounding a courtyard.

'What does it look like inside?'

'An ordinary courtyard with a well and benches.'

'How many doors from the courtyard into the building?'

'Four.'

'Who lived there?'

'The teacher and his family.'

'Large?'

'Two wives and nine children.'

She went on with the story and I could see the scene more vividly, fifteen girls between eight and twelve in white blouses and dark-blue skirts, most of them with their hair plaited or tied tight at the nape of their necks, attentive and serious, some of them so small for the chairs that their legs in their knee-socks and black buckle shoes did not reach the ground. The teacher wore a white jellaba and skullcap; a solemn man who taught slowly and painstakingly. He had set up a blackboard on a wooden easel and wrote while he spoke, wrote and wrote until the board was completely covered, and then he rubbed everything out and started all over again, talking and talking, writing and writing. Behind him some of the girls became restless, two put their arms round each other's shoulders, one yawned, another pair were giggling. The teacher noticed none of it, he was too intent on his teaching.

'What did you think about?'

'The sort of things you think about at that age.'

'And what were they?'

She smiled, leaned a little closer, her voice becoming richer. Eleven of the girls were already married, but still living with their parents. When they were strong enough to carry two water jugs on their heads they would go to their husbands' houses.

She was quiet after she had told me that. We sat in silence watching the sunset. Her brother picked a blade of grass and stuck it between his teeth.

'And you?'

'My mother and my fathers wanted to wait. Twice a year a district nurse used to come out to the island for a week; mother had confidence in her.'

'But now she's decided?'

She nodded.

'I'm grown-up now.'

The cargo boat had gone, and the line between sea and horizon had faded in the encroaching darkness. The school and the meeting house and all the other buildings seemed to shrink in size, and a voice was calling from the house. We stood up and let her brother precede us, which seemed to surprise him, but he made no comment. She squeezed my arm before going on ahead of me, walking quickly.

'Have you been promised in marriage?'

She made no reply, but her back seemed to spread in the

darkness between us, swaying the way the backs of women with water jugs on their heads have swayed for centuries in this country, and suddenly I knew what it was like to be on a rusting cargo ship setting course for an empty horizon.

Her father had slaughtered a goat and was standing in the little front garden roasting it when we came back. He had made a spit of branches and was rotating it slowly, while the flames licked up the blood on the carcass and rose blackened and sated into the night sky. Melted fat dripped on to the fire and sent showers of sparks out into the darkness. Her brothers fetched more wood, her mother and younger sister stood at a table cutting up vegetables, onions and olives for the first course. She went and stood beside them and was given a knife, a bowl of sweet potatoes and a brief, friendly instruction; she nodded and started dicing the sweet potatoes. I went over to the fire and her father. He smiled and moved slightly to one side, as if to make room for me.

'Have you got plenty of time?'

'Yes.'

'Good. There are so many of your race who haven't.'

He smiled again and basted the goat carcass, pouring a red liquid over it from a mug. The carcass sizzled and sputtered.

Yes, I have time to wait for her, because that's what you're asking me, I know.

He took a drink from the mug and held it out to me enquiringly. I took a swig and swallowed it, looked at him and took another. He laughed softly under his breath.

'Allah didn't let the vines at the back of the house give us grapes for them to rot.'

The two brothers arrived with more wood; they glanced at their father and he nodded. They disappeared into the house and a few moments later we could hear music from a cassette player. Behind us the lights had been lit in the houses on both sides of the street, small squares of light. Her father took another drink from the mug and passed it back to me.

'Are you all right financially?'

'Yes.'

Down by the harbour a car hooted, the cassette player in the house was turned up, the three women by the table were laughing, and suddenly there were noises all around us; I could hear my own heart among them, yes, my finances are all right, I can put down a deposit on the dowry if you decide that's what you want.

'What do you do for a living?'

'I write.'

'That's good. What do you write?'

'About my travels. And you?'

'I work in the olive grove and the vineyard these days. I used to work in the post office. A long life, and now it's over. There's so much that's over.'

He glanced towards the women at the table as he uttered the last sentence and gave a little sigh. The mother and two daughters were chatting as they prepared the food, telling stories, laughing and shouting.

'The old has to give way to the new; it's sad, but that's how it's always been. Come on, let's carry the meat across.'

I helped him to lift off the spit and we bore it between us. The mother watched us as we came over to the table and he met her gaze. The little sister put cushions on the ground in a circle and brought us round the water to wash our hands; her mother placed the four dishes of the first course in the centre and handed out maize pancakes for us to break and use to pick up the food. Everyone sat down, even the women, though before the war they would have eaten separately. The family talked amongst themselves and sometimes to me. The crickets were tuning up in the darkness, some neighbours called in at the gate to exchange greetings, the conversation speeded up, and I ate and pursued my own thoughts and enjoyed the starry sky. I heard a faint voice and turned my head to try to make out what it was saying. I saw a figure, a black silhouette against a golden desert, saying something to me, gazing at me, wanting something from me. I tried to concentrate on the meal, but the desert figure was pulling me away. The first-course plates were taken into the house, the father carved slices off the roasted goat and laid them in a basket, the mother fetched a bowl of salad and a basket of bread. We opened up the flat bread, leaned over and filled it with slices of roast goat and salad. Our eyes met over the food, she sitting between her mother and sister, catching my eye and holding it until her mother spoke, then looking away, but I knew she had noticed: we were sitting eating with her family for the first time and my mind was elsewhere.

The desert figure grew larger, the voices of her family and neighbours faded further into the background, the voice of the desert figure came closer and closer. It was a woman, the voice husky, but it was a woman's voice all the same. I tried to make out what she was saying, but couldn't. I wanted to get up from the meal and go out into the darkness to listen properly. After a while the figure turned and went, the golden sand drifted over her footprints, and once or twice she glanced back at me over her shoulder.

'No, mother.'

I awoke from my reverie and looked at her. Her voice had an edge to it. She had risen from the meal and her mother was staring at her with a furious expression in her dark eyes.

'Dance.'

'No.'

'A daughter doesn't say no to her mother.'

'This daughter does.'

16

Her mother beckoned one of the brothers over with her eyes still fixed on her daughter. She pointed at the house.

'The cassette player.'

The brother went indoors hesitantly and reappeared carrying it a moment later. The mother waved her hand again and said something and he fetched a tape.

'Dance.'

The gentle rather plaintive tones of a flute came from the cassette player, with a stringed instrument and drum in the background.

'Dance.'

Her voice was peremptory. The daughter folded her arms over her chest and just stood looking at her. The two women assessed each other's strength for several seconds while the rest of us sat in silence. It seemed as if the crickets were trilling louder than before and the stars shining more brightly. Then the mother turned to the father, still keeping her gaze on her daughter, and uttered a few words I couldn't understand. The father mumbled in reply: it was clear he wasn't going to get involved. The mother got angry and shouted, the father didn't respond.

Then something happened. That's one of the sides of her character I like best: she doesn't adopt inflexible attitudes. She suddenly bent down to her mother, put her arms round her and started talking. Her voice was conciliatory, as if she wanted to break out of an impasse. Her mother looked up in surprise, unsure of herself, a little afraid even, and asked a question. Her daughter replied. The mother said nothing, the daughter took her in her arms, gave her a hug and went into the house. She came back out with her rucksack, searching through it as she walked, opened a cassette and inserted the tape in the machine. I was interested to see the expressions on their faces, father and mother and brothers and little sister, when the first notes sounded. They turned in wonder to the cassette player, listened to the bass and the guitar and the drums, tried to find their way into the unfamiliar rhythm.

Bob Marley and reggae beneath a sky of twinkling stars against a background chorus of crickets, the black outline of an island against a dark sea, the smell of roasted goat and the heat from the fire. She took off her uniform jacket and began to dance. She was wearing a white T-shirt and dancing with slow movements, not sensual, not provocative, but elegant and joyful. She closed her eyes and smiled, hummed along, stretched out her arms and clicked her fingers on every other beat. Her mother followed her with her eyes, taking in every movement as if to keep her under control, but also more than that. A group of neighbours stopped to watch, leaning on the gate. Her mother spoke sharply to them, go away, but they grinned and responded amiably. The expression on her mother's face changed, a fleeting shift, loss and fear, profound fear, but also pleasure, and something else, which I couldn't find words for until one of the neighbours by the gate spoke, and she turned to them with a glance at her daughter, and I saw that it was pride. The daughter went on dancing and after a while caught her sister by the hand and dragged her up. The little girl looked questioningly at her mother and her mother waited for a moment and the universe stopped and held its breath until she nodded and smiled. The girl called out and one of the brothers increased the volume, the other brother joined the dancing and I heard feet tapping over by the gate. Her mother turned back to me and asked, 'Is that your father singing on the cassette?'

'Yes.'

She smiled again, this time at me.

'He sounds nice. Bring him with you one day and we'll slaughter a goat for him.'

★

18

They took us to the evening market after the meal, a billowing chaos of stalls and overhead tarpaulins down at the harbour. The paraffin lamps under the green awnings threw long shadows that expanded and contracted, and they transformed the stallholders too: they were people with shadows, not people without. I looked round and saw that everything had a shadow; the aroma of roasted nuts, the clucking of chickens in a cage, the loud cries of the vendors – all cast a shadow. We walked among the stalls by rank, first her father and I, then her two brothers; then her mother with one daughter in uniform and another holding her hand. We drank tea under an awning, we paused to inspect spices, dried fish and fruit, we smiled at everyone who tried to sell us gold watches. Local pop music blared from stalls only a few metres apart, and the two brothers managed to get in a few dance steps before their mother made them desist.

Were we a family? Was she a daughter who had come home with a man, or was she a stranger who had come on a visit with another stranger? By some benches where two men lay sleeping, unshaven and snoring, she met the first of her childhood friends: she was pregnant and had two half-grown boys with her. The two women called out and embraced, and I could see the contrast between them, in their eyes, in their faces, in their bodies. The others evidently saw it too and were quiet. The two friends went through names, or tried to, and I realized that it was soon entirely one-sided, it was the pregnant woman who was doing all the talking, about this friend and that. Whenever she asked a question it was just met with a shake of the head, it was the policy of this liberation movement never to disclose the identities of the fallen or the wounded or the missing, it was the policy of this liberation movement never to give information about troop movements or operations, not in the past, present or future. In the end the pregnant woman gave up. Instead she went on recounting stories herself unbidden, about the girl at the back of the class who had fallen in love with the butcher's son and married him and now had five children and they were just as much in love; about the one with the pigtails and the thin face who had left for the mainland to go to university; about the one with the bad knee who had been married off to an older man who kept her locked in most of the time. She was a good storyteller; her dialect was strange to me, but I could follow everything she said anyway: when she described pregnancies she did it with expansive, proud gestures; when she spoke about love she put both hands against her cheek and beamed; when she said how many and how big her children were she picked them up with a smile and patted them on the head.

I could see something was going on beneath the dark-green-and-brown camouflage uniform, some slight deflation, or perhaps more as if a candle had been lit, but flickering rather than burning bright.

I went down to the bench in the olive grove the next morning and sat and watched the island waking up. A few lights were visible here and there, the muezzin was calling to prayer from the minaret, somewhere a cock was crowing. The island seemed gradually to emerge from the sea as the night lifted, dark at first, then grey, finally in colour. The arch of the sky rose higher and higher; in the beginning there was light, and the light was as red as flames, and the horizon extended in two directions, further and further. After a while I heard her come walking down the path and moved over to make room for her to sit beside me. She had been crying and did not speak immediately.

'It wasn't entirely as you imagined it would be?'

'Not entirely. I thought they would be more pleased to see me.'

'They were. But you've obviously changed a lot.'

'So have they.'

We went on sitting there in silence. I watched her studying the island, its slow arousal from its nocturnal sleep and its morning stretch towards the new day, and I could see the memories brush her cheek and bring a little smile to her eyes. She looked towards the school and the mosque and the market, the meeting house and the social centre and the Council of Elders house; she was holding them up like pieces of a jigsaw puzzle, a life, trying to see where they belonged.

'Is it possible to forget your own roots?'

'Many have tried.'

The muezzin was calling to prayer again, and for the first time I saw her pray. She took off her uniform jacket and spread it out like a prayer mat, her white T-shirt taut over the muscles of her back as she knelt and bent to pray. I followed her movements with my eyes and had a feeling of watching someone who was very close to me and yet at the same time very far away. Every time she prostrated herself in prayer it was as if she disappeared from something, from something to do with us, and a cold breeze blew in from the sea.

'I feel as if I don't have just one past, but two, this and the front. If they can't be reconciled, I'll have to choose between them, choose one and forget the other. Is it possible for people to forget?'

I didn't reply, but stood up, returned to the house and fetched my writing book, which was like my notebook, only four times the size. She looked at it as I came back, drew her uniform jacket more tightly around her and leaned against me, gazing out at the sea and the horizon while listening to me reading about oblivion. She sat absolutely still, and I saw her gradually disappearing into what I was reading, disappearing from the island and sea and horizon and slipping into an undulating golden desert landscape.

Timbuktu is eight desert nights from the place where I know I shall find her, eight desert nights behind a camel, beneath a sparkling sky, eight nights in complete stillness. Timbuktu is the natural place to start a journey into forgetfulness, from forgetfulness to oblivion; once centre of the Islamic world, the seat of architects and scientists from all the Islamic lands, gathered together by a succession of Mali kings, with twenty-five thousand students at the university. Nowadays bleak and deserted and partially buried in the sand and ignored in the timeless everyday life of North Africa, where today is all that exists; yesterday has gone and will never return and there is no one who knows anything about tomorrow. The architects and scientists have vanished and only the camel drivers in the marketplace are still there, with little glasses of tea and strings of beads and dirty jokes. I set off from the town in the evening and know that what I am leaving is the epitaph for an epoch; every night I travel it will disappear further and further into the distance until I can hear it no more, and I start to look towards the horizon, towards the meeting of heaven and desert, eager to see what is awaiting me. Is it an epitaph or a resurrection?

On the eighth morning a figure appears, shimmering in the strong light, a hazy, irresolute figure in dark desert clothes. It stands half turned away from me as if in defiance. We are the only people there, the horizon encircles us desolate and empty, but the figure stands averted, as if waiting for me but at the same time not wanting to admit my presence.

I stop some metres away, take off my rucksack and put it down on the sand.

'Who was it?'

She was holding her hand over the page to stop me.

'A Russian woman writer and Islamic Sufi.'

'That can't be right. A woman? A Sufi is a man.'

'Isabelle Eberhardt was both. She maintained that the male Sufi set her free from her femininity and gave her power over her own life, the power to write.'

'What do you want with her?'

She still held her hand over the page.

'To find out what it is about her that fascinates so many people. Since her death nearly a hundred years ago one biography after another has been published, more and more frequently in the last couple of decades. Is there something about our own times that attracts us to a person like that? Some call her a seeker of oblivion, the word she herself uses about her nomadic brothers in intoxication. Others describe her less generously: worn out by the age of twenty-seven, no teeth, no breasts, no menstruation: given up to a life of intoxication and self-destructive sexuality.

She sat there letting the words sink in. I could see traces of them in her eyes. Then she removed her hand from the book. I went on reading.

> I pull out a skin water bottle and pass it to her. She drinks, hands me back the bottle, nods to me to follow her, and moves off. I screw the top on the bottle, hoist my rucksack on to my back and follow, walking ten metres behind her.
>
> At Touggourt there is a roadblock, a French officer and four soldiers sitting in the shade of a tin roof. The officer wants to know more about her, his eyes wide with astonishment when she tells him she is Russian and Muslim. People whose only wish is to escape the desert never understand why anyone would come here voluntarily, she whispers to me. I get through with no problem, almost as if I don't exist, as if the French soldiers hardly see me or only see parts of me.

We sit in the old quarter of Touggourt playing cards until two in the morning, when it's cool enough to start out. We ride all through the night and don't get there until eleven next morning. Bir Sthil has good water but difficult guards. She has a fever and a thirst. At nine in the evening we set off again. In the middle of the night we meet a man and a woman being escorted to the oasis by an armed African for a divorce. We continue the journey together. Early in the morning we take a rest. We carry on after an hour or two and reach the next oasis, only to find that the French gendarmerie have orders not to let her stay there more than twenty-four hours.

She speaks fluent Arabic and is dressed as a man, and she prefers the company of men; I don't know whether she is aware that they perceive something feminine about her and are attracted by that. We travel at night and sleep by day, spending the evenings with camel drivers and land workers over bitter green tea in small cafés. She converses with them easily and naturally, with just an occasional brief glance at me.

At another roadblock there is the first sign that things are not what they should be. The officer checking our papers tries to pretend he doesn't know who she is, tries to be chivalrous and Gallic, but his warmth is overdone and not entirely convincing. Twisting in the saddle a few metres further on, I see him hurrying towards the command tent, probably to write a report and send it by courier. I turn back round and look at the woman riding beside me. Does she know that the French colonial powers are using her, that they let her associate with the Sufis to learn more about them? And if she knows, does it affect the image she has of her own freedom?

Kenadsa in the grey light of dawn, a handful of houses scattered around a well, two dark palm trees, a fire and music from an open doorway. The music reaches out to us, first coming to meet us, then following us, a slow melancholy tune from something that sounds like a harmonica. I raise myself in the stirrups in an attempt to resist it. I have the same feeling as before, a long night of travelling through the desert where everything is black, shades of black, and then the first glimmer of grey far off, and the outline of houses and trees, closer and closer, and then the music, signs of life. Riding out of the darkness of the desert into an oasis with lights is one thing, riding out of the darkness of the desert and into an oasis with music is something quite different, because the music of an oasis is always melancholy. People in an oasis know something about life that others do not, and they express it through their music. I remain standing in the stirrups; I know that if I sit back down in the saddle the melancholy will take hold of me, and what will happen then, what will happen then? I know what will happen: I will get no further, because that is what is so melancholy about an oasis, that there is no reason to leave it.

I can see she has been here before, many times. She knows exactly where to go and hardly looks about her. When she greets people it is with familiarity and without surprise, the way people greet each other when they are used to meeting.

She stops in front of a little house of sun-baked bricks and tethers her horse to a post. The house has no windows and a carpet covers the doorway. I can just make out a light behind the carpet, but only dimly, as if the house is trying to keep the light to itself. I tie up my horse beside hers, and she calls out in the grey darkness;

a boy comes running, she gestures towards the horses and gives him money. He nods and disappears, she pushes the carpet aside and beckons me in. There are three men in the house, half sitting, half lying on reed mats; their clothes are in tatters and their eyes empty. None of them looks up. We do not seem to be interrupting any conversation: all three give the appearance of having said all they have to say. I put my hand on the arm of the woman by my side and ask, 'Will you describe this room for me?'

She removes my hand from her arm before replying.

'Partially ruined, lighted by day by a single eye in the ceiling of twisted and smoke-blackened beams. The walls are dark, ribbed with lighter-coloured cracks that look like open wounds. The floor is of pounded earth, but it is soft and dusty. Seldom swept, it is covered in refuse.'

We sit down, but still none of the men looks up.

'The place is a shelter for desert vagabonds, for nomads, and for every sort of person of dubious intent and questionable appearance. It seems to belong to no one; as at a disreputable hotel, you spend a few badly advised nights here, and go on. It is a natural setting for picturesque and theatrical events, like the antechamber of the room where the crime was committed.'

I listen to her voice, which has something dreamlike about it, and I look at what she is describing. The room is empty except for a reed mat and some cushions. On the mat stands a chest which serves as a table. I note the signs of life: a fresh bunch of flowers in a vase of water, a copper kettle on a tripod, two teapots and a large basket of dried Indian hemp.

'Kif smokers require no other decoration, no other *mis-en-scène*. They are people who like their pleasure.'

'What do you mean by that? Doesn't everyone like their pleasure?'

She pauses before answering, demonstratively patient.

'Kif smokers are travellers who carry their dreams with them, carry them across the countries of Islam, worshippers of the hallucinating smoke. The men who meet here are among the most highly educated in the land.'

She points.

One of the men pulls out a collection of pipe bowls, wiping the mouthpiece on his tattered jellaba. She sits down, I sit down by her side. The three men talk to one another in low voices, looking across at us from time to time. She is in Arab attire; she has removed her fez and shaken out her black hair, making her face look vulnerable. She says something to the three of them, they look at her in surprise and take a few moments to respond.

Pipe after pipe is lit and passed round between the five of us; water gurgles in the bottom of the pipe stem. The smoke of kif hangs in the room, its sweet smell unmistakable. When one pipe is finished, one of the men picks out the glowing ball of ash and puts it in his mouth. He sits with his mouth tightly closed while he fills another, then he takes out the ball of ash and uses it to light the new one.

She leans over to me. 'See, he can't feel it burning him.'

'But it burns him; it's just that he can't feel it?'

She doesn't answer, but I think the distinction crucial: nobody can avoid being burnt by life, but some have distanced themselves so far that they are no longer aware of it.

One of the men starts clapping his hands, lazily, in a

steady rhythm, and the other two join in. One clears his throat of kif smoke and sings, a tentative ballad with slow movements and a melancholy undertone. Another raises his hands, holds them up in front of his face and recites something, the same sentence again and again, as if he is trying out different ways of expressing it.

'What is he saying?'

'The unspeakable anguish of pleasure crushed them both beneath its weight.'

'Who?'

'Two people who fell in love.'

I lean against the wall and close my eyes, trying to envisage the anguish of pleasure. I imagine it as a rock of black lava lying on a mountainside waiting for someone to feel pleasure, waiting for someone suddenly to let out a little cry and start jumping in the air for joy. Then the rock would come tumbling down the mountain like an evil eye, thundering downwards to strident trumpet fanfares, crushing their pleasure, crushing all who feel joy. I can see it hurtling towards me, I try to move but cannot, I try to heave myself up from the floor, but cannot.

'Open your eyes.'

She is shaking me. I press my hands to my eyes and force the lids open. The three men have lain down, still intoning words and tunes, but more languidly now, at longer intervals, an eternity between each hand-clap. Finally they lie completely silent, just staring at the flowers. What is in them now? Ecstasy? Emptiness? She is whispering in my ear.

'They have reached the magic horizon; now they can build their dream castles and fill them with pleasure.'

As I fall on my side I manage to shout, 'Don't do it, don't do it, they'll just be crushed.'

But my voice is no longer heard, it has no sound, it has

become a white ribbon fluttering across the room. The ribbon slowly twists into a spiral and within the spiral a sentence is rotating: Over the years I have learnt to expect no more of life than the ecstasy oblivion brings. It hits the walls in its spiral and curls up, forms itself into a coil and then straightens out again, and I can see groups of words bumping against the edges of the white ribbon: 'Over the years I have learnt to expect no more of life than the ecstasy oblivion brings.' The walls quiver, as if in the wind; I turn round and see that the sentence is coming from the woman by my side, she is holding the white ribbon with a blue glass hand and blowing the sentence into a spiral, again and again: Over the years I have learnt to expect no more of life than the ecstasy oblivion brings. And through the hole in the roof a white light is streaming which makes first the contrasts and then us disappear, and I just have time to think, forget or be forgotten, before everything turns white.

A horse is galloping, I try to get up, how can I hear a horse when everything is white, I close my eyes and see a man seated on a bench at the top of an island reading to a woman; she is sitting with her head on his shoulder and a uniform jacket tight around her, and he is wearing black trousers and a grey shirt with two breast pockets. Above them a falcon is circling: it listens to what he is reading and nods to itself, wheels out over the sea and comes back to hear more. I open my eyes and am filled with whiteness, the man and the woman on the island disappear, as do the falcon and the sea. I close my eyes and am back with them again, she has taken his hand and is holding it to her lips, I can see tears in her eyes but he can't, he is sitting reading something he obviously doesn't want to read; he seems troubled, and avoids her gaze. I try to call to him, but he doesn't hear; I shout louder, in tears myself, 'Can't you

see, can't you see?' but he doesn't see. I open my eyes again, the whiteness streams in and blots them out, I close my eyes and am back with them again, open my eyes, close them, open, close: 'Over the years I have learnt to expect no more of life than the ecstasy oblivion brings. I suck oblivion in, a deep draught, fill myself with whiteness, they have gone now, or I have gone, it matters not, oblivion is the key to the riddle of the oasis.

'Why did you want to meet her?'
    'To study oblivion.'
    'Why?'
    'I don't know.'
    'Do you think she succeeded?'
She clasped her arms round her legs and rested her chin on her knees while she waited for an answer.
    'To be quite honest, I don't know.'
    'Why not?'
    'Because I have a feeling that she romanticized. I'm always a bit sceptical of people who romanticize.'
    She closed her eyes.
    'What does it mean to forget?'
    'To move on.'
    'Where?'
    'In your own life.'
    'And you don't feel that she moved on?'
    'No. I think she ran away.'
    'Isn't that the same as moving on?'
    'Yes, but not in your own life.'
The island had awoken. The blue sea had returned and the turquoise sky, the straight horizon and the colours of the houses had returned, and the green hillsides, the sounds of the ferry loading down in the harbour and the men chatting on their way to the olive groves.

She put her hand on my arm and asked, 'Tell me what it is that draws you to her.'

'Her language. She adds something to what she describes. I don't know whether it's acceptable to do that, but she does.'

I brought out a paperback bearing her name.

'Listen to this: "The farmers are singing as they work. The pale wheat, the brown barley, lie piled on the earth's flanks, and the earth herself lies back, exhausted by her labour pains."'

She snuggled up to me.

'That's strange.'

'Yes, it's strange. Even when she writes about terrible things she writes lyrically. It's as if atrocities become music and desperation becomes dainty steps in a ballet. Listen: "One morning the melancholy rain ceased to fall. There was a shuddering in the essence of things. Little by little the colourless sky was killing everything. The sky arched above like a vast ironic smile. From all the villages scattered across the countryside rose great cries of despair."'

I was flicking through the pages and reading extracts to her. I had marked certain passages in the margin. She sat in silence, concentrating on my words. A falcon circled above us.

'If you were to describe our war in her way, what would you say?'

'The red hour of the evening when all goes quiet.'

'Be serious.'

'I am serious. Even people dying she describes in colour. The thought of death is perhaps easier to accept when it's described like that.'

She hugged her jacket even tighter around her, as if to protect herself from something. I knew what it was.

'It doesn't happen like that.'

'Not in your world. But maybe in hers.'

★

31

She took the paperback with the maroon cover from me and traced the author's name with her finger. I-SA-BELLE E-BER-HARDT. She was learning the Latin alphabet and I was not sure whether I liked it; I knew it would open up a world that would change her. I looked at her henna-stained nails as she held the book and turned the pages. Daylight had come, down at the harbour someone was chipping rust off the hull of the ferry, and her fingers cast shadows on the white leaves. I put aside my writing book and notebook and leaned back, leaned back and waited. I knew she would find it, she had a special ability, it was as if individual words called out to her and grabbed her, as if they radiated something, a light, a colour, something she could see and hear without understanding. Sometimes she would take the notebook out of my hands and look at what I had written, and when she asked me to translate a section it was always the most painful, the most difficult, never the trivial. Now she was leafing through a paperback with a shiny maroon cover and came to a halt at one particular page.

'What does this say?'

I took the book from her. The hammer blows from the harbour sounded louder and more resonant, metal on metal.

'"Already she was no more than a vaporous vision, something without consistence that would soon be absorbed by the clear moonlight. Her image was indistinct, very far away, scarcely visible. Then the vagrant, who still loved her, understood that at dawn he would be leaving, and his heart grew heavy. He took one of the big flowers of the spicy camphor tree and pressed it to his lips to stifle a sob."'

'Did he really do that?'

'Yes, it seems so.'

'It must have been awful for him to leave her and travel on when he still loved her. Scarcely surprising that his heart grew heavy.'

I made no reply. She reached for my hand and put the paperback in it, folded my fingers round it and said, 'Where in the book does it say why?'

'Why what?'

'You know what.'

I thumbed through until I found the page with the unedited notes and read:

' "Vagrancy is deliverance, and a life on the open road is the essence of freedom. To have the courage to smash the chains with which modern life has weighted us (under the pretext that it was offering us more liberty), then to take up the symbolic stick and bundle, and get out." '

I stopped reading, but kept my eyes on the book. I could feel her looking at me, sense her drawing back a little to see me more clearly.

I first met her in a café between a beach and a town; on one side of the café wooden boats painted green, blue and red were drawn up on the beach, on the other were paved streets with cars and low houses. I liked it there halfway between the ephemeral and the eternal; I could alternate from one to the other just by turning my head. She worked in the café and followed me with her eyes, held my gaze when I looked at her.

As a rule I was the only customer, with now and then a few tourists who would arrive on the morning boat and eat a meal in the beach café before leaving again on the afternoon boat; quiet married couples in their fifties. One evening an American came in wearing a voluminous blue shirt and khaki trousers, close-fitting at the ankles. He wanted an American beer and someone to talk to. He tried me first, without success, and then her. He talked about himself, about his work, about his thoughts: he ran his own business putting on courses in self-development and positive energy, fifteen hundred dollars for three days; everyone has large reserves of unused energy within themselves and he made a living by teaching people how to release it in a positive way, how to make contact with energy reserves in others and achieve a synergistic effect, harmonious creativity. He looked at her with dewy eyes and said he could feel there was energy streaming from her, but it was dispersed, and he could help her focus it, make it positive, if she would tell him a bit about herself. He glanced quickly over at me as he asked that.

She came from a part of the world where people don't waste words, a part of the world where people carve their houses and steps into the rock instead of building them on top. I think that says something about the character of the people: some carve themselves into the world, others abstract from it and reconstruct it.

She waited a while before answering, opened another bottle and set it in front of him before beginning to speak.

'When I was born my father cut steps for me from the house up to the top of the cliff, to right where the cliff face drops vertically into the sea. I was his first-born and it was important for him to build something for me; that was a way to channel his pride. The steps were to be my path to God, and when I climbed them I would feel myself getting closer to the light with every step, until I stood at the top and had light on me from all sides.

'My mother used to talk about how he would work on the steps by night. He worked in the landowner's olive grove all morning and all afternoon, he made love to my mother all evening, and he worked on the steps all night. He had a little lamp with him and my mother would watch its glow getting higher and higher every night. She would hold me to her breast as she listened to the rhythmic beat of father's hammer and the sound of stones tumbling down into the water. From time to time my father would turn and wave to her, and she could just make out his shadow against the cliff. Sometimes he would wave to the top of the cliff, as if to God. One night he tried to wave to both my mother and God at the same time as he was hammering, which was not very clever, because his aim was so erratic with all the waving that he hit himself on the hand and let out a horrific scream, and my mother dropped me to the floor in fright at the scream and God was so angry that he pushed my father off the cliff. My mother saw a great hand come down from the sky and push him from behind, pouf, never seen again, and what would happen to the steps?

'As was the custom among my people, my father's brother came knocking on the door the next evening, and mother said only if you finish cutting the steps. It took three brothers and six children before the steps were finished, and every evening when mother kissed us goodnight after evening prayers she whispered, "God bless you, my children, and never take His name in vain, especially when you're in an exposed position."

'And so one day the steps were finished. We stood and watched my new father cut the last step and cautiously lift the lamp over the edge; the light was steady in the darkness up there for a long time and then it floated backwards in an arc, very slowly, and my mother scratched another mark on the wall even before the light was extinguished in the sea. "That's the end of him. Tomorrow you can climb the steps to your God, my dear."'

'And that's what you did?'

The American gazed at her in eager anticipation.

'Yes.'

'What was it like?'

'Like climbing steps.'

'What did you feel?'

'Feel?'

'What were you thinking in your mind?'

'Thinking? I was climbing steps.'

'And what was there at the top?'

'A Coca-Cola machine.'

'A Coca-Cola machine?'

'Yes.'

'Can that be true?'

'Why should I lie about it?'

Her eyes were on me as she said it, and I knew I had fallen.

That was in the middle of a journey. I had rented a room in the town for a few weeks. When the journey resumed, there were two of us.

We didn't meet in a beach café, we met at the front, in a trench, he with a notebook and pencil in his hands, me with an automatic rifle, 7.62 calibre. There's a side to him that unnerves me: he has started editing his own life. He doesn't rewrite it, he doesn't lie, but he changes it just the same. 'Can we rewind and erase that?' he once asked, and I laughed happily. Only now have I begun to feel that that is exactly what he does. The beach café happened, and the American happened, but only much, much later. In the beginning was the front, and the front was with God, and the front was God. He was wearing black Levi jeans and a worn grey shirt with two breast pockets. He jumped down to me in the trench and greeted me. I liked him immediately, his eyes, his voice, the way he jumped. My mother used to say that you never know a man until you've seen him jump, and really not until you've seen him fall, but then it's generally too late.

I first met him at the Zal am-Shiva front. I was on watch, it was late afternoon, hot and still. There were four of us on watch in the upper trench, in two pairs, and the valley before us was completely quiet. We had been warned of an armoured attack and we were waiting. Suddenly we heard voices behind us and turned round, and there he was with the commander. They jumped down to us in the trench, both trying to hide the fact that they were not as agile as they used to be, and he came up to me with a smile. I raised my rifle and let off a burst right into his smile, smashed it into little pieces and heard the commander yelling. No, no, no, I didn't do that, I fell on his neck in slow motion as I closed my eyes and gave up, let go, I can't go on, and my tears ran down onto his shirt as he stroked my hair and said there, there, there. No, no, no, I didn't do that, and nor did he: he crouched down beside me with his forearms on the parapet and his chin resting on his hands, his right elbow just touching mine, and I could smell his aftershave lotion and thought, Allah is mighty, aftershave in a trench. He came back the next day smelling again of fresh aftershave, and I turned towards him and suddenly knew something about him, that he took care of himself even in a trench. That's knowing quite a lot about a man. The day before I had known almost nothing, just that he had looked at me and smiled and smelled of aftershave, and that I didn't move my elbow away from his.

His voice matched his smile and his eyes. I listened to its melody and knew that he came from that part of the world where the land and the people are covered in snow for half the year and people have to sing to one another, not talk, because words get lost in the snow, but notes do not; I touched him gently on the shoulder and saw that he was aware of it, and pointed out two tiny tanks on the other side of the valley. He followed the direction of my finger.

'How sweet they look.'

'They put them out while they're still small.'

I tried not to say it, because I knew that something would happen the moment I did, but I couldn't help myself and it happened, he recognized it, I could see that in him, and later on, as we lay next to one another in the constricted bunker listening to the explosions of grenades, I could hear his heart and knew that he could hear mine, and I realized reluctantly that a bond was being forged between us, and the whole of our mutual story is the story of that bond, for the bond of fear is different from the bond of love. That was before I realized that our meeting on a journey was a matter of chance, not of necessity, irrespective of the fact that we were both travelling; before I realized that he and I were travelling in two diametrically opposed directions: I was trying to travel away from fear, he was travelling towards it; I was trying to change things, he was content to study them. I came to understand later that it was himself he was studying, and that he would be an incomplete person if he stopped travelling. I remember that I once asked him about it.

'Can people be divided into two types: those who want to change things and those who don't?'

'Definitely.'

'Can one who wants change live with one who doesn't?'

'Hard to say.'

Sometimes he is easy to talk to, other times not. That's how men are. A little later, when we were enveloped in wordless intimacy, he moistened his finger in his mouth and drew letters one by one on my breast, watching me to see whether I understood: a subject changes its object just by defining it. But has anyone thought of the fact that the act also changes the subject?

There had never been anyone who had written that on my breast before.

He read something to me one evening, something of his own. We were sitting on the deck of a boat with our backs to the rail watching the sun go down. I wrapped my burnous round my head and shoulders and snuggled up to him. It was a mild evening, a gentle breeze, calm sea, the sound of the engine rising and falling, rising and falling. I was asleep and was woken by a gradual awareness of him sitting writing in his notebook, a simple little spiral-bound notebook that he always carried with him; I knew that what he was writing had something to do with me.

'Couldn't you read it to me?'

He would almost never read me things he had written himself: that was one of the rooms he kept locked; and he would never read while he was writing: that room was firmly shut.

'Don't ask anything, don't move, just read it to me.'

I stayed as I was, close against him.

' "Running Deer? Must you go?" '

'Who is speaking?'

'A young woman. She has long auburn hair and fear in her eyes.'

'Where is she?'

'She's standing on the stage in an amphitheatre with the audience on three sides. There has just been an incredible amount of activity on stage, noisy, wild, exuberant, and now silence has descended on both stage and audience.'

'Read on.'

' "Running Deer? Must you go? The leaves are falling from the trees, the moon grows pale, the time of frosty nights is approaching. The colours are vanishing; will you vanish too, Running Deer? Will your children listen for your voice in the wind, look for your eyes in the sunset? Why can't the white man take the land he wants? Great Spirit has not said the forests and prairies and mountains are just for us, Great Spirit has given us the forests and prairies and mountains for us to live, Running Deer, not to die. The white man also needs to live. The white man doesn't travel; when he finds a place he likes he puts up fences round himself and stays. We don't need to stand at his fences staring at what he has taken, we can travel on to all the places he has not taken, to all the places where there is singing and dancing. Great Spirit is not behind fences, he is outside. Must you go, Running Deer? Will it be you who does not return this time? Swift Wolf and Silent Falcon did not come back last time, their wives live with their brothers now. Are

43

you giving me to your brother, Running Deer? Bear Claw is a good man, but living with Bear Claw instead of with you would be like hitting a badger when aiming at a stag. Don't you understand that the white man always takes back double what he gives away? Don't you understand that for every white scalp you bring home, he will take two of us?" '

'Is there more?'

'Just one line.'

'Read it.'

' "Must you go, Running Deer?" '

I don't know whether it was his voice or his shoulder or what he read to me, but something struck a chord in me. I listened to it and could not be sure whether it was painful or sad.

'Did he have to go?'

'Did you?'

That was the only time I had asked to be admitted while he was writing, asked to know what he was writing as he wrote it, and I knew that it changed everything.

———

She asked me to read something to her one evening, something I had written while she was asleep. We were sitting on the deck of a boat with our backs to the rail, and she was sleeping. I sat gazing towards the land, experiencing the sensation of distance, of freedom. The deck was packed with people, chickens and pigs, but remarkably quiet nonetheless, as if we were all aware of the same thing, something cathedral-like. The piece I was writing was isolated from any context, but that didn't worry me, I knew the context would come later.

'Can you read it to me? Don't ask anything, don't move, just read it to me.'

Her voice was close to my ear. I don't like reading to

anyone while I'm writing, it's as if butterflies are hatching from my pencil, playful, questing, shimmering butterflies, and if anyone tries to catch them, they die. Now I suddenly saw where my text was coming from and where it was going; it was like quantum physics: a photon changes direction when it is observed, the universe changes when a human being looks at it.

As I read I heard the sound of the words spilling on to the deck and on to her, now completely silent; her breathing was no longer audible and her heart had stopped beating, she was sitting absolutely motionless, listening. I put out my hand and laid it on her cheek, but withdrew it, since the touch was a betrayal of what was happening; I was releasing the butterflies from my notebook and she was catching them, and neither of us will ever go back to a time before that.

She sat with the Koran in her lap reading aloud to me. I lay on the ground by her side facing her, so that I could see her eyes and the night sky as she read.

' "And when God shall say, O Jesus, Son of Mary: hast thou said unto mankind, Take me and my mother as two Gods beside God? He shall say, Glory be unto Thee! It is not for me to say that which I know to be not the truth." '

She marked the place with a slip of paper, Surah 5, before closing the book. We had pitched camp on top of a flat cliff with a view over eternity, an endless plain with no horizon, just a still band of silver in the middle, and a high heaven with blue stars. She sat with her head on my shoulder, as she usually did when something was difficult. We sat in silence and listened to the universe, which was revolving slowly and expanding. She opened another book, turned a few pages and read.

' "If God wishes to bring about the creation of a child, an angel will say, Lord! Man or woman? Oh Lord! Cursed or blessed? What will his profession be? What age will he be?

45

The angel writes all that down while the child is in its mother's womb." '

'That's not in the Koran. It's part of the oral tradition in the Hadith, Bukhari.'

'It's sacred all the same.'

I knew what her difficulty was: she had had a letter from her mother, about me, about the man who had been chosen for her at home.

She asked, 'Do you think that everything that is going to happen to us is written?'

'What do you think?'

'I was brought up to believe that.'

'And now?'

'The years at the front have changed me. Did we win because God wanted us to, or because we trained harder and believed in what we were fighting for?'

'Be careful now.'

'And if we won because God wanted it, why did He allow it go on for thirty years and let fifty thousand of us die?'

'You see what I mean.'

The moon hung big and bright over the plain below us and was reflected in the river, the starlit sky making it look unreal, as if it were hanging in thin air. She felt for my hand.

'Why don't you have any religion?'

'Because I haven't found any answers to the questions you've just posed.'

'Can't you see that this is a problem for my mother? If you were a Christian, it would be different, then she could have told the neighbours that you had the wrong beliefs, of course, but at least you believed. But not believing . . .'

The sentence spread its wings and glided out from the clifftop. I watched it go, shimmering, soaring away from us in leisurely flight, not believing, I could hear the words, not believing, they had an echo, not believing.

46

'When are you going to ask me about the letter from my mother?'

I stroked her hair.

'She's compared our horoscopes. They don't agree.'

'But the foreman of the olive grove?'

'The cigarette vendor. Agrees.'

Way down below on the plain a drum began to beat, ragged, unfamiliar, as if there were five or six beats to the bar. She stood up and took my hand.

'Come on, let's dance.'

She put her hands on my shoulders and gazed into my eyes as she danced, and I knew what it was that had drawn me to her: it was her eyes, or something in her expression, something that gave me a feeling of wanting to let myself go. She smiled.

'Don't count the beats, just follow me.'

She started humming as she danced, humming and gazing into my eyes and smiling; she came closer, pressed her forehead to my lips. The universe expanded above and around us, the murmur of the drum rose and fell on the plain below, I breathed in her scent, of aloe and tamarisk.

Later, when she had gone to sleep, I took out my notebook and wrote:

'I have learnt never to underestimate the fatalism of her people. It is the same with Christian determinists and Jewish cabbalists, but they are marginal even in their own society of belief. In her people fatalism is fundamental to their belief. Strictly speaking it is not right for a Muslim to weep at a funeral, because it can be taken as a criticism of God's judgement. Here a person dies only because God has decreed that he shall die.'

She was lying with her head on my lap. I looked down at her and continued writing.

'The Koran has a verse that in principle admits freedom of

will, Surah 18, 28: "Let him who will, believe; and let him who will, be an infidel." That provides support for those who find it difficult to accept that God punishes or rewards them for deeds for which they are not responsible. At an early stage in the Islamic religion the learned men tried to suggest that God determines only the character each individual is born with, but that was a view that never caught on, probably because it was not concrete enough. In the tenth century Al-Ashari formulated the solution that still prevails: All actions are created by God, and man is free to appropriate those actions.'

She moved, and I closed my notebook and laid it aside. A mist had covered the plain below, looking as if it had grown out of the ground. I felt her breath on the back of my hand; there was an intimacy in it that was good. God has created all deeds, even the evil ones, and man is free to choose, but those who choose wrongly are punished, because in her people's religion it is obedience that counts, not belief; obedience to God, to the clan, to the one who has given you life.

———

The mullah was the same as before, only more so. He smelt worse and talked louder, his voice and his eyes wavering.

'What do you want?'

He used to give us instruction behind the curtain in the mosque. His body had grown fatter, but his hands were the same.

'To talk.'

'About what?'

'My family.'

'A woman does not talk with a mullah about her family. Fetch your father.'

There was dust on everything in the room. In a rack on the wall was a rolled-up prayer mat, and next to it a microphone.

It was said that he liked to touch himself while he called to prayer.

'My father is dead, as you well know.'

'Then fetch the man who provides for your mother.'

'He doesn't decide about me.'

'Woman!'

Halima had been whipped by him once, before she was fully grown. He had tied her up with her own clothes and read from a book of Hadith before he set about her with the leather whip. Halima said later that the scar from his eyes took more time to heal than the scars from the whip.

'The man who provides for my mother has taken money for me in advance. His tongue is no longer free.'

'Then fetch your eldest brother.'

Ibrahim, Ibrahim with the dark, sad eyes and soft hands. Ibrahim who was always laughing, who was always so easy to communicate with, right up to the day I whispered to him that I was leaving. Now he led me back to the mosque, holding two of my fingers firmly in his grip. The mosque was down by the harbour, we had to descend all the steep alleys, and I noticed how light he was on his feet, how strong and handsome.

'What does your sister want?'

The mullah had made tea. Ibrahim took the glass he was offered and put it down without looking at me.

'Permission for *mutah*, to marry another.'

'*Mutah* is for divorced women and widows.'

'She says she is a widow. After the war.'

The mullah was silent. That was the only good thing people had to say about him, he knew when to keep quiet.

'Who is he?'

'A European. Of high caste.'

'Of our faith?'

'No.'

49

'But he will convert?'

Ibrahim with the soft hands stroking my hair outside the mosque while the mullah went on shouting behind the door he had just slammed, the soft hands and the low voice asking is it him or is it you who won't? And the mullah suddenly opening the door and yelling a hundred lashes, woman, a hundred, and two women stopping and spitting before continuing on their way. Ibrahim put his arm round my shoulders and took me with him, producing a handkerchief and giving it to me without saying anything.

'Where are we going now?'

'To a marabout.'

'Are you just as strong in your faith?'

He didn't reply. It was the first time I had been alone with him since coming home, the first time we had walked together; I took his hand and intertwined our fingers, squeezed hard. I could hear him toddling by my side, smiling as he tried out his first words; I could hear him singing by my side with a fishing rod and a catch of fish in his hand; I could hear him jumping by my side with his schoolbooks bouncing up and down in his stiff leather satchel. I turned and looked at him, a young man, with a young man's fingers and a young man's eyes, and I knew that something had come between us, something that both bound and divided us.

'What's he doing?'

'Washing.'

We passed the chair maker and the car mechanic and wended our way towards the centre, at the head of the harbour. The marabout was in an old warehouse right by the market. The nearer we got to it, the more yellow hands there were above the doorways in every street.

'Surely Fatima's hand used not to be in so many places before?'

'It was you who used not to be here.'

He sounded annoyed, as if I had touched upon something sensitive.

'When did the Evil Eye come?'

'It's always been here.'

'Ibrahim, Fatima's hand doesn't keep the Evil Eye out, it keeps it alive. Belief in the Eye comes first, then belief in the hand.'

'Was that what you learnt in the war?'

He was walking ahead of me, as used to be the custom. I took his arm, he speeded up, I ran along behind him.

'When did the marabout come?'

'While you were away.'

'The first part of the time, or in the middle, or the last part?'

'In the middle.'

In that case he had been here for some long while. Ibrahim tried to jerk himself free, but I tightened my grip on his arm and prevented him, put my arms around him from behind and hugged him, placed one hand on his forehead and pulled his face against mine as I slipped the other hand down his jumper. Laughing, he tried to wriggle free.

'What's this?'

I held up a small leather amulet. He would not look at it.

'When did you start wearing a verse of the Koran round your neck?'

'When you went away.'

Ibrahim, Ibrahim, with the dark, sad eyes and the soft hands and the low voice, the little boy who stood in the window and watched me leave, in the dead of night, while all the others were asleep; I could see him now, see what I didn't see then, see him standing in the window until I disappeared from view, see him creep into the living room and pick up the Holy Book, tear off the corner of a page and write my name on it in big uneven letters, see him cut out two pieces of leather from his satchel and glue them together to make an amulet. I put my lips to his neck and kissed him.

He stood completely still.

'People don't do that here.'

He didn't try to move away. I dropped the amulet back inside his jumper, took him by the hand and walked on.

'Nor that either.'

'Ibrahim, the marabout is new for me, and I am new for you.'

We reached the marabout's warehouse. There was an enamel sign on the door: *If anyone turn away from his Islamic religion, kill him. Hadith. Bukhari* 89, 2.

Ibrahim gave an apologetic smile and tapped on the door. A voice called out in response, and we opened the door and went in. The warehouse was big and dark and full of smoke, and something else, something I recognized but could not place.

The marabout, a shrunken, dried-up little man, lay on a mattress of sacking. Above the mattress he had built himself a low ceiling of cardboard, as if he wanted to make the space seem less. At his side the Holy Book and an overturned radio. I observed it automatically, and only then did it occur to me that I had begun to notice things the way he did, and immediately I knew what else was in the room that I had not been able to place. It was him, he was there following me with his eyes. I could hear our lecturer in political theory saying it was historical realities that laid the pattern both for the individual and for the development of a society, not religious beliefs, but it was not the lecturer I could see, it was him; he was standing there in his black jeans and his worn grey shirt, his notebook and pencil protruding from his left breast pocket, gazing at me with an expression I could not interpret.

Ibrahim and the marabout were talking to one another in low voices beneath the cardboard roof, looking across at me from time to time, and I felt anger rising in me, anger because they were talking about me as if I were an object, anger because without thinking I had waited by the door.

There was a carpet hanging on one of the long walls with a lamp above it, showing the direction of prayer towards the Black Stone. All around it hung simple paintings with quotations from the Book; one of them was Surah 2, 173: 'O believers, retaliation for bloodshedding is prescribed to you: the free man for the free, and the slave for the slave, and the woman for the woman.' I felt a new surge of anger: this was not what we had fought for; what we had fought for was for something quite different.

Ibrahim was gripping my shoulder, and I realized that he had been speaking to me and I hadn't taken it in.

'Can't you hear what I'm saying?'

'Sorry.'

'The marabout wants to know when you first became aware of the jinn'.

'What jinn?'

'The ones that have got into you.'

A swallow swooped up into a corner of the roof, probably to a nest there, and a ray of sunshine in white dust cut obliquely through the room down to the marabout's cardboard world. In the distance I could see him taking his notebook and pencil out of his breast pocket, almost as a reflex; he knew this was important, that something important was coming now, and what came was my scream: 'There are no jinn that have got into me, that's not why I'm making the choice I am, I'm not going to change my mind however much you try to drive the jinn out!' I screamed and screamed and screamed, I felt the scream welling up from my feet, but I could tell from the voice that it was a little schoolgirl who was screaming, in a dress and pigtails, and when she had finished screaming, a teenager took over, thin and gawky with long arms and legs, and she screamed with tears of rage and desperation in her eyes, but the marabout did not hear it, the schoolgirl and the teenager were too far back to be audible. The marabout was muttering exorcisms as he tied amulets round my neck containing verses from the Holy Book, and Ibrahim with the dark, sad eyes stood silently looking on, and in the distance I could hear a notebook being closed, like a reality being shut out.

'Ibrahim, don't talk to me about a jihad.'

At last I had got my own voice back, at last I could hear myself yelling.

'The great jihad, not the little one, that's over.'

Ibrahim was holding me by the shoulders and shaking me. I could see the marabout behind him; he had sat down on the mattress and was watching us. He was wearing a tattered robe with a black cord belt, and had long straggly hair and beard.

'Our war wasn't a religious war, it was a political war.'

Ibrahim was about to shout something in reply, but did not have time: the marabout suddenly jumped up from the mattress, tore down the cardboard roof, rolled it up into a megaphone and put it to his mouth.

'Woman! Do as we say!'

His voice was surprisingly deep and powerful. I had not expected it from such an unkempt man. He came up closer until the other end of the roll covered my face: 'Woman! Turn aside evil with that which is better. And say, O my Lord! I betake me to Thee, against the promptings of the Satans; and I betake me to Thee, O my Lord! that they gain no hurtful access to me.'

The marabout took the megaphone away from his mouth and in a normal voice announced to the empty warehouse, 'Koran, Surah 23, 97–100.' Then he put the tube of cardboard up to his eyes and stared at me through it.

'Woman. We were against you going to the front at all. Don't come here and tell us what's what.'

Then he gave me a shove with the cardboard and knocked me over.

As a boy I worked with plywood a lot. I liked the word, plywood, I liked the material, I liked working with it. First I would cut out characters from my comics, and then paste them on to sheets of plywood, and finally saw them out with a jigsaw, carefully tracing the outline with the blade until they stood before me as solid figures.

It was some time before I realized that was exactly what I was doing with her. I took her with me on my travels, I spread out map after map in front of her and pointed. What do you think it's like there, and there, and there? No travel accounts exist from there, we'll have to go there ourselves if we want to know what it's like. She looked up at me and smiled, looked down at the places I was indicating and her face took on a remote expression.

Was she robbed of her dreams at the front? Or did she just pack them up and put them away, keep them locked in a cool, dark place? I don't know; all I know is that she was robbed of her years as a young girl and a young adult woman – instead she had years as a young soldier and a young adult soldier.

Does a soldier dream?

I felt that in one way or another she found her way back to something in herself when we travelled together. She became brighter, happier, more direct; more overt in her feelings. It was as if she went back in life and fetched what had been stolen from her.

She was easy to be with then; she always was, but easiest then. Until it occurred to me that I was at my jigsaw work again: I was cutting her out of her life, pasting her on a journey and sawing her out very carefully until she stood there as a solid figure, in a place where neither of us had been before. Her background, her culture, her family were missing; her personal history, her choices in life, her natural reactions were all missing.

Is it possible to live with a plywood figure?

Is it possible to live with a person who cuts you out of your background?

When I understood what I was doing, I learnt a lot about her and a lot about myself. When the journey is the goal, everyone becomes transient. I wrote that sentence on a piece of paper I had with me, and I would take it out occasionally and look at the last word, listen to the sad, dismal sound of it.

———

His journeys have something contradictory about them, something as much loved as hated, as much forced as voluntary. He gets angry when anyone tries to romanticize the life of the nomad, yet is always on the move himself, always on the road. Every departure is a fresh start, and every fresh start contains the possibility of winning and the possibility of losing. I think that's what compels him to travel, the risk. Staying put is safe and secure, travelling is dangerous. I have written 'Stay if you can, travel if you must' on a leather amulet and tied it to his upper arm with a strip of snakeskin. He hasn't read it, but I know he knows what it says, and he knows that I know. We both know it would not be him if he stayed, but someone else, and would I want that person?

For me travelling is the same as fighting, and the war is over now. The war robbed me of my girlhood years, it stole my years of young womanhood. We were travelling for years on end, from one front to the next; we gradually freed the country from the grip of its occupiers, gradually shaped the country and the people who lived there, made them plough, build roads, hospitals and schools. What we did not understand was that we also created a distance between them and us. We made them shape their own reality the way we had shaped ours, and we were divided: they stayed, we went on, and if we ever returned, it would be as strangers.

He was a different person when we were travelling together. Not different in himself, but a different person. Or was he the person he was all the time, and it was just that I had to see him on his travels to discover it? I remember he read something odd to me once, something he had come across: ' "When a traveller comes to a new town, he finds his way back to something in himself, something he had forgotten he had." '
    'What does that mean?'
    'I don't know.'
    'What is it in himself he finds his way back to?'
    'Something he had forgotten he had.'
    'In a new town?'
    'Yes.'
    It was only on journeys that he made notes about himself, as if he could see himself then. And when travelling he had plenty of time at his disposal. It was as if everything else ceased to exist when he was travelling. I remember once we were sitting on a bench on a station platform waiting for a train. We had been there for quite a while and he had bought us something to drink; it had been a long, hot day full of new impressions, and we were sitting in silence watching the sunset.
    'I wish I could sit on this platform with you for the rest of my life.'
    I didn't need to look at him to see whether he meant it, I knew that he meant it, and not because of the way he said it,

because he hadn't said it in any special way, he had simply said it. No, I knew that he meant it because of who he was.

Who he was now?

If he was a different person when we were not travelling, why was that so? Was it because of me? Or was it something about the act of travelling that brought out this other person in him? Was he finding his way back to himself?

I couldn't always be with him, that was impossible for me. Would there come a time when he reverted to travelling alone? Would that be my final image of him?

———

Rome, where tranquillity is relative and reflection is framed by magnificent historical architecture; my base and workplace, the centre of my European web. A two-roomed apartment in a quiet side street close to the centre, second floor; from the windows I could see across to another block of the same period, with elaborate ornamentation and a café on the corner where I sometimes sat alone with a drink in the evening. There was a bakery on the ground floor of my block, I went there every morning to buy fresh pastries to have with my coffee, and every single day I paused as I came out of the shop, opened the paper bag, inhaled the aroma and smiled before going on up the stairs. I went down again half an hour later, crossed the street, headed towards the centre, bought a newspaper, skimmed the headlines, rolled it up under my arm and walked on. My office was right in the city centre, the traffic in the street outside so dense that it looked as if the cars tooting their horns were actually parked. When the lorries that took out the nightly deliveries of newspapers from the printer's returned in the morning, the drivers had to wind down their windows and yell to get into the gateway through the queue of vehicles.

My office was decorated in pastel shades with airy curtains; a fern stood by my desk and shelves full of books entirely covered one wall. There was a window on to the street, windows to the main editorial office on a third wall and on the fourth a painting of the head and shoulders of a white woman, her eyes closed and a red spot of blood on her forehead.

One morning he didn't go down to the bakery for fresh pastries. Every morning when I was staying with him I used to stand at the window watching for him to come out of the shop, his sniff of the fresh pastry, and every time he would look up at me and laugh and make discreet signs to me to cover my breasts, and every time I would smile back and shake my head. Bare brown breasts make Italian men clean windows: never were windows cleaned so assiduously on the other side of the street as when I was standing there, and anything that gets Italian men to clean windows is good.

Rome, where both contemplation and bare breasts are framed by magnificent historical architecture, and one morning he just got up and put the coffee on, just wrapped himself in his kikoi and lit the gas. He sat down on the bed by my side when he brought in the two cups and handed one to me. I tried to imagine what a European woman would have said, surrounded by all that magnificent historical architecture, when she realized that something was wrong, seriously wrong.

'You're thinner.'

Not that anyway.

'Leave me alone.'

He tried to remove my hand, but I pulled it free and laid it back on him. European women may do as they will, but I like to see my hand on his chest and stomach. I could tell that words were coming, it was just a case of waiting: I could hear them foregathering inside him, beneath my hand, almost as if they were alive. I could feel them fighting for position, but were they struggling to be first or last?

'The editor called me in yesterday.'

So that was it.

'He's worried about me.'

Him too.

'He wants me to write about other things.'

He was looking at me, as if inspecting my eyes for a question, a 'what?' that could have saved him, but this time he would not escape. I put my other hand on his back and pressed, one hand on his stomach and one on his back, and could hear the words screaming in panic inside.

'Why is he worried?'

He didn't answer.

'Did he start by counting up how many wars you've covered for them in the eight years you've been there?'

Still no answer.

'Was it for once not enough to say you stopped counting at ten? Did he go on counting anyway? Or did he reckon up five trips a year to wars and famines, sometimes the same ones, sometimes new ones, multiply by eight and make it forty?'

I pressed him hard and sudden between my hands and squeezed three words out of him: 'Not at first.'

'What did he say first, then?'

'He read aloud something I had written.'

He turned his head and looked me in the eyes; I put my fingers to his lips and helped the words out, gently, so that they could speak what his editor had read out:

' "Below the road is the beginning of the refugee camp, the largest in the world, and in the middle of the refugee camp is the press camp, fifteen little tents spread out inside a thousand-square-metre enclosure cordoned off with barbed wire and armed guards. Outside some of the tents are tables and chairs and food, beer, brandy.

' "Refugees crowd around the press encampment on all sides; they stand unmoving with their fingers through the barbed wire staring at the foreign journalists." '

Then he stopped reading and turned away.

'What did he ask you?'

'Which side of the barbed wire I'm on.'

I wanted to put my arms around him and hold him, but didn't dare, for fear of stopping him talking.

'What else did he say?'

'He asked about my state of health. My office has one wall with windows in it facing the editorial floor and he has started putting a cross in his diary every time he sees me sitting with a woollen blanket around my shoulders in a centrally heated room kept at twenty degrees. He counted up the crosses from the last three months while I was there and asked what the matter was.'

'What did you say?'

'The shivers. Malaria. Tropical fever. Does it matter?'

'Did he ask about your eating disorders? About the times when you can't stand the sight of meat? Did he ask about the diagnosis from your last hospital admission? The one you forgot to tell us about? Did he ask about your fear of going to sleep, your fear of the nightmares you know sleep will bring?'

He took one of my hands in both of his. I waited. No more words were forthcoming. I withdrew my hand.

'What was he worried about?'

I waited, and was on the point of repeating the question when the words came.

'He's afraid I'm losing my faith.'

'In God or mankind?'

'Is there a difference?'

He took my hand again.

'He asked what the opposite of a nightmare was. I said dreams. It was the right answer. So much for writing that piece from Kenadsa, the dream of oblivion. He wants me to travel and write about dreams, mankind's dreams. A dream for every nightmare, one dream journey for every war.'

He smiled.

' "Ne'er a pleasure without a pain." '

I hit out at him.

Later, when he had been down and bought the pastries, he took me over to the map of the world on the kitchen wall. 'There, and there, and there are our collective dreams.' But I noticed his sidelong glances at other places on the map, at the nightmares.

'What if you'd said no?'

'There's a temporary vacancy on the sports desk. Synchronized swimming.'

When he had gone off to the newspaper office I took a chair over to the window and sat down. The street was comparatively quiet in the mornings, a few pedestrians, a few cars. I whispered the phrase first, *let them die*, just let them die, let them slaughter one another if that's what they want to do, tell them to phone when they've finished. I spoke the sentence once more, half aloud now, *let them die*, just let them die, and I felt a pang: we needed him before, others needed him now, he was one of our keys to foreign aid, he was one of those who reported what was going on, but he was also mine, and I didn't know how long I could go on seeing him go away on journeys to others, *let them die*, just let them die, let them slaughter one another. I was shouting now, and a woman down on the street stopped and looked up. I pulled my head back from the window, wondered what kind of pressure his editor had put him under but checked myself. It's not pressure to say to a reporter that if you want to go on writing about wars you must also write about dreams; that's not pressure, that's advice, and it suddenly struck me with a jolt that the pressure must be coming from elsewhere.

I stood up and closed the window, put on my sandals and went out. What was uppermost in my mind now I had to say by a fountain, I couldn't bear to say it in a closed room. I walked till I found a little park with a circular fountain, the water pouring down into the pool from a bowl held aloft by three marble angels. I took off my sandals and lowered my feet into the pool, looked into the cascade of water from above, and said, 'I am with a man who has to be forced to put a brake on his self-destruction.' The angels looked down in alarm and I nodded; they exchanged glances. 'I am with a man who has to be forced to put a brake on his self-destruction, and the pressure is coming from within, not from without, the pressure is coming from himself, he is agreeing to write about dreams in order to be able to continue covering wars,' and I shouted out my sudden insight: 'There's something religious about his relationship to war, he's made a pact, a pact he can't escape from.'

'Have you sketched a plan?'

The editor was looking at me enquiringly.

'Yes. Dreams. Not wars, not famines, but dreams.'

We were sitting in his office with the window open, the smoke from our cigarettes drifting out of the window into the clear autumn light.

'What sort of dreams will you go after?'

The editor's gaze lingered on the smoke as he waited for a reply.

'Humanity's collective dreams.'

'Which are?'

'Oblivion, freedom, immortality, power, riches, a fresh start, peace.'

'And where will you go?'

'To the places the dreams relate to.'

'What places are they?'

'Mythical ones. Humanity has passed down its collective dreams as myths. You just have to follow the tracks: Timbuktu, oblivion; Mandalay, freedom; Babylon, immortality; Samarkand, power; Cuzco, riches; Patagonia, a fresh start; Shangri-La, peace.'

'Tell me more.'

The editor pulled out a notepad and unscrewed the cap of his fountain pen.

'In Babylon early man erected a pillar up into the sky to put to the gods the only question he wanted to ask: why the gods had created themselves immortal and humans mortal. Mandalay was the hub of the Buddhist universe, the very dream of freedom, freedom as religion. Samarkand was the capital of the Mongol territory, the most powerful kingdom the world has ever known. In Cuzco Europeans found the Incas' gold and lost their reason. Shangri-La is the dream of peace within ourselves and with others, a peace where conflict, ageing and death do not exist and nor consequently does evil. Timbuktu is the dream of oblivion, of leaving behind, forsaking.'

'And Patagonia?

The editor looked up.

'The dream of a fresh start. Right at the end of the world, as far away from everything as it is possible to get. Patagonia has for hundreds of years drawn people who found it necessary to burn their bridges behind them. All their bridges.'

The editor numbered the places and drew little circles round the numbers while he thought. Then he screwed the cap back on his pen and said, 'There's one dream you haven't mentioned.'

'The dream of being seen?'

The editor nodded.

'If we are, in contrast to the gods, mortal, isn't it natural to want the utmost from life, our brief little life? Isn't it natural to want freedom, riches, power and youth, isn't it natural to want oblivion, to forget that we are mortal? The existentialists say that man is the only living being that knows he will die, so we can never be happy, yet happiness is after all what it's all about for most of us, happiness in this life, not in the next, and for some life can get so difficult that the only escape they can see is to burn all their bridges and start again, somewhere far, far away. But in the midst of all that, running through it like an undercurrent, we dream of being seen, and what is it we dream of then?'

'I thought this was a Catholic newspaper?'

'What is it we dream of then?'

'The body. Baghdad. A Thousand and One Nights.'

The editor smiled and leaned back in his chair. He clasped his hands and looked up at the ceiling and said in a soft voice, 'I want you to start there, I want you to tell me the dream of the body, and while you're about it I want you to tell me why the allies go on bombing, day in and day out, without the world appearing to show any interest.'

> In Baghdad there is a small family hotel behind the big central fruit and vegetable market. It is run by an Armenian with a Lebanese wife and two solemn teenage daughters. It has twelve rooms, four on the ground floor and eight on the first. The rooms on the ground floor open on to a large communal room with two groups of armchairs and four little breakfast tables. Under the second table from the wall someone has written with

a green ballpoint pen *frog, millpond, the frog jumps, the sound of water*. I would probably never have seen it had not breakfast one morning been interrupted by a sudden violent boom that sent everyone running for cover under the tables.

'It's American bombers!'

The Armenian was dragging his teenage daughters out from under the third table as he shouted. They had sought refuge there with some Mexican boys. The man at my side shook his head in annoyance. 'No it's not, it's the UN.'

He had short hair, green khaki trousers with pockets on the thighs and straps round the ankles, a white T-shirt, and a pudgy face with broken veins on both cheeks. He had introduced himself at breakfast as a German weapons inspector from the UN. He spoke bad German.

'Iraq is being bombed because of its arrogant refusal to comply with countless UN resolutions and its continued production of weapons of mass destruction, for ignoring human rights and threatening its neighbours.'

'Like Israel.'

He looked at me in surprise, as if he wasn't sure whether he had heard aright.

There was another explosion. The table and the weapons inspector in the green trousers shook. The first bomb to fall in an attack always has something unreal about it, the next turns unreality into an inferno. I pointed out the Haiku verse under the table.

'Bashō, seventeenth century. The whole universe is in that sound of water, including Buddha's teaching.'

I crawled across the floor past the third table that was sheltering the Mexican boys and on to the fourth where a British woman and a Saudi-Arabian businessman were crouching. She was in her mid-thirties with black shadows under her eyes and a low-cut jumper. His mouth glinted with gold teeth.

'Please don't stare down the front of my jumper.'

Her voice was deep and slightly husky. She caught my eye as she spoke.

Another explosion, a shower of plaster off the walls. Bomb number three will kill you; bomb number one is a chance, bomb number two a possibility, bomb number three a certainty. The Saudi-Arabian businessman took a mobile telephone with gold casing from his belt and keyed in a number. The woman watched him in disbelief.

'What are you doing? Put that telephone down at once!'

Her voice had risen to screaming pitch. The businessman regarded her dispassionately as he held the phone to his ear to wait for an answer.

'Don't you know that mobile phones disturb the electro-magnetic fields?'

'So what? Are they your fields?'

The businessman still seemed totally indifferent.

'No, but the carrier pigeons are mine.'

The woman was so angry that she was sobbing. She threw herself on him and ripped the phone out of his hand.

'Give me my phone back!'

The Saudi bellowed. It seemed to come naturally to him. The woman sat back against the table leg and grinned triumphantly.

'Woman, give me my telephone!'

The Saudi sprang up so fast and aggressively that he banged his head on the underside of the table and fell on top of the woman. She shrieked and stuffed the telephone down between her breasts. It disappeared almost entirely, just a glimpse of gold discernible a long way down. The Saudi thrust his hand with its long black hairs and signet ring into the neck of her jumper.

'Rape! Rape!'

The woman's voice was shrill. The Saudi turned towards the other tables and shouted as he fumbled beneath her clothes, 'She's taken my mobile phone!'

Another explosion shook the room, glasses clinked and plaster cracked, heads nodded in sympathy.

'Get your hand out of my jumper, you swine!'

Her voice was hoarse and nasal. She rose on all fours and butted him with an involuntary grunt. He raised his free hand to his lip and stared at the blood on it, still groping for the mobile phone with the other. It must have slid right down, because more and more of his arm disappeared into her clothing and her eyes suddenly opened wide.

'Don't touch me there. Just don't touch me there!'

She butted him again, once, twice, three times, with the same short cry each time. He tried to hold her head away but couldn't. The blood was no longer seeping from his lip, but pouring.

'That's for the four I lost in the Oxford-to-Newcastle.'

She butted hard, as if to punctuate her words.

'And that's for the three I lost in the Manchester-to-Cork.'

New punctuation. One of the Mexican boys under the next table called across to me in a low voice, 'Hey, gringo, what was it she lost?'

'Her homing pigeons.'

'Oh.'

The Saudi now had hold of the woman along the whole length of her body under her clothes, and he lifted her up and turned her over on her back. She was butting her head into thin air and groaning.

'Hey, gringo, what's that got to do with him?'

'He uses a mobile phone.'

'Oi, oi, oi.'

The Saudi lay on his stomach across the woman's face and shoved his other arm inside her jumper.

'My mobile phone!'

There were half-smothered yelps coming from the woman.

'Hey, gringo. We've been discussing it and come to the conclusion that her pigeons get scared and fly away when anyone uses a mobile under her jumper. Is that it?'

The Saudi was now lying outstretched on top of her and hunting for his phone around her stomach and thighs. We could see his hands moving beneath her clothes.

'Nearly. The pigeons navigate by electro-magnetic fields, and mobile telephones disturb those fields. So it's become almost impossible to hold pigeon races. In a single race in the USA fifteen hundred out of eighteen hundred pigeons got lost; in another two thousand disappeared. One man lost thirty-four of his thirty-seven birds and said he had nothing left to live for.'

All went quiet under the next table. The Saudi gave a sudden howl and turned towards us in joyful triumph: he had found his phone. Decisively, he withdrew his arms from the woman's jumper, pulled down the zip of her trousers and stuck in the hand with the signet ring.

'Hey, gringo. Pigeon race?'

'Yes.'

FREEDOM

R ome Termini station and the taste of pride, different
from the taste of joy. Eighteen platforms full of people
and a loudspeaker voice driving them before it with curt
raucous announcements, and the taste of pride as she descended from the train, sharper than the taste of joy, more
precise; pride that it was me she was waving at and heading
for.

'Have you been here long?'

'Since yesterday.'

She smiled and took me by the arm. We moved off into the
stream of people, let it flow past us and round us like an island –
that was the picture I had of us, together we made an island – and
stopped on the steps outside savouring the chaos. Rome is best
seen from there, from the steps in front of the railway station:
right there is the perfect balance of sounds and smells and visual
impressions that made me stay. Bawling street vendors, screech-
ing car tyres, the smell of heavy summer rain and the redeeming
exuberance of the architecture. We went to our usual café and
ordered espressos; that was a ritual every time she came to visit
me. We walked in silence down the main street and into a side
street to our favourite café, in her silence; European silence is
almost always loaded, her silence almost never, and it makes me
feel secure. We walked in the silence she possessed, arm in arm,
our faces turned towards life, and I took in details I hadn't seen
before, nuances of colour I hadn't registered.

She started talking as soon as we had sat down, telling me –
with her eyes, her hands and her shoulders – how things had
been. I knew a lot from letters and telephone conversations,
but now I could see her in it, hear how she was. She told me
about the evenings at school and the nights with her course
books, she told me about her mother who was ill and needed
her, about her bad conscience, about everyday life at home,
about neighbours quarreling, neighbours drinking, about the
mosque and prayer, and through what she said she also told
me something else, I could hear the sound of it, faint and
rather indistinct, but loud and clear when later we stood with
our elbows on the windowsill watching the light withdraw
from the city.

Rome Termini and the smell of skin, the taste of oblivion. We
stood at the window watching the rain, I with my elbows on
the windowsill, she standing behind me. She had her arms
round me and her chin on my shoulder; I could feel her
breath, hear her heart. She slipped two fingers under my shirt
and started stroking me, came a step closer. Rome Termini, I
could see the light and hear the sounds above the roofs of the
houses on the other side, Termini, there was something finite
about the word, something final. She began to sing softly into
my ear, and her fingers beneath my shirt were stroking me to
the same rhythm. It was a song from her homeland: I hadn't
heard it before, but I recognized the language.
    Rome Termini and the taste of oblivion that proximity and
skin induce; we could stand for hours and days, months and
years just looking at the rain. For me nothing else existed then,
absolutely nothing: the rain washed away everything that had
been, the afternoon, the evening and the dry sunshine; while
it rained, rain was the only thing that existed, nothing else,
and it was impossible to imagine that it would ever stop
raining and that the world would take shape anew. I put my

head out of the window as far as I could, turned my face up to the sky and drank in the rain; it was like drinking forgetfulness. She laughed and pulled me back, wiped the rain off my face and hair and held me tighter, rested her chin on my back and rocked me gently to and fro. It was only us then, not even the room around us existed, just us and the rain, neither of us had a past, and the moment would never end.

Sometimes she brought a herbal unguent with her. She always let me sniff it first, and told me what herbs were in it and where they had been picked. The first time I asked what kind of effect it was meant to have, but she didn't answer, just looked at me as she knelt down and took hold of my hand. She dipped a finger in the ointment and began to rub it into the palm of my hand, concentrating carefully. She followed the life lines and stroked them out, she followed the prediction lines and stroked them out too; I could feel the warmth of the unguent and thought I could see a light. She was kneeling in front of me and massaging light into my hands, first one and then the other, and I bent forward and laid my brow against her head, breathing in the scent of her and of the moment, and she held her head absolutely still. When she had finished, she always leaned back a little and gave me a look I couldn't interpret, a look that rather frightened me. She would take my right hand and place it behind her neck, curving my fingers until I had her neck in my grasp, then she would jut her chin out, tilt her head back and close her eyes. Never was I so captivated by her as just then, at that moment, and somewhere deep inside me I understood that the unguent had nothing to do with me, but with us, that she was anointing the hand that was to touch her.

'Will you write about this?'

She whispered it, right up against me.

'I don't know.'

'Yes you do.'

75

She held me tighter.

'Sometimes I have the feeling that things aren't real for you until you've written about them.'

'Maybe.'

'It seems as if that's where you travel to, into what you write.'

'Maybe.'

She held me at arm's length and examined me, stroked my cheek, ran her fingers over my lips and I had a taste of the unguent. Then she put her head on my chest and blew gently, and I saw that it was stardust she was blowing out, white, glittering stardust, that covered me like a sparkling quilt, and she smiled and whispered, 'Now I can see you.'

———————

He was with us in the final assault on the town by the sea that had once been white, the one with the summer palace. We had bombarded the town for three days and nights, hour after hour, and with every shell we exchanged glances, because we knew the town was also full of civilians, but this was the last battle in the final offensive. My comrade fighters had nodded when the reporter arrived, as if they had been expecting him. They gave him tea and bread as was our custom, and he talked to them as was his, and I believe they knew he had seen me where I lay in a machine-gun emplacement a little further along, and I believe they knew I had seen him. But they were pleased he dropped in on them as well, and they showed it by wrapping a dark cloth round his head, since a white head was easy to aim at, and he thanked them by asking what the devil they had done with his palace, and they doubled up with laughter, and I think that laughter was what we needed to dare look again at the palace, because we had a feeling we had committed an act of madness, incredible madness, and then we dared raise our eyes from the palace ruins to take in the rest of the town. Eventually he thanked them for the tea and bread and moved off to see me, soldiers at several points reaching out to touch him and saying something, and he smiling in return; they watched his progress until he was lying by my side in the gun emplacement and I was fondling the hair on the nape of his neck, twirling it round my finger as I spoke.

The rainy season had just ended and the acacia trees were in full bloom, the ground smelt fresh, the sun was still gentle and the sea was like a gigantic mirror. The attack was to be launched in the morning, in military terms not the most desirable time; we normally attacked at dawn, but the hour had been chosen out of regard for the civilian population and would also give us an element of surprise.

My unit and two others were intended as decoys. We were to advance on the town before the main offensive, cross the flat land in three lines separated by a distance of a hundred metres and run for cover as soon as we were fired on. The decoys' function was exactly that, to get the enemy to open fire and so reveal their positions. It was a high-risk and high-status operation.

He didn't move when I gathered the unit about me; his arm was on my back and when I raised my hand in a gesture of command it suddenly felt as if the hand belonged to both of us. The others wriggled across to us, with complete acceptance. The commander shouted a warning before we stood up; he shouted as we stood up, fully aware, I believe, that it was too late but at the same time aware that he had to shout. We jumped up out of the machine-gun emplacement, I in camouflage uniform, he in black trousers and a grey shirt with breast pockets, I with an AK 47 at the ready, he with a camera in his right hand and a notebook and pencil protruding from his left breast pocket. The rest of the unit sprang up and ran behind us, one after another in a line, presenting the smallest possible target, and a hundred metres away on both sides the other units were doing the same, but not the two of us. We were running side by side, and it was only after several paces that I realized we were running in step, as if one were a mirror image of the other. Now we could see how devastated the town was, how savagely the shells had blown in doors and windows and walls and how mercilessly they had demolished roofs; and I thought that it wouldn't have looked so bad if it hadn't been white, I associate white with something special, something that shouldn't be destroyed. And suddenly I felt we were no longer running towards the town to attack it, but to save it. We reached a large rock and he threw himself down behind it while I ran on. I reached a field of tree stumps, dropped down and beckoned him forward, and thus we approached the town, in what is called advancing by rushes. I kept him covered with my rifle, he covered me with his eyes.

We were waiting for the sound of shots, the sharp, mocking crack of a shot that would change everything; we were putting our heads on one side and listening, running, covering each other and listening until we made it to the edge of the white town, and then suddenly we stood up to our full height and simultaneously raised our arms and ran forward. We could hear a sound now, it was the sound of voices, hundreds of voices weeping and laughing and shouting and screaming, and following the noise came the sight of men and women and children and young people running towards us and suddenly we all realized there were going to be no shots, that the war was over, and the cry that arose from us swept across the plain towards the crowds streaming out of the town, and I tore off my camouflage jacket as I ran, swung it twice round my head and threw it away, running on in a short-sleeved white T-shirt with my arms outstretched.

I looked back and saw the soldiers behind me do the same,

they ran towards the town stripping off their uniform jackets and shouting, and suddenly the plain was transformed into a billowing white pattern on a deep green background, re-minding me of a war cemetery, and we were now surrounded by weeping and laughing people wanting to embrace us, to touch us, and somewhere drums began to beat, fast, jubilantly, and I held out my arms and took a few dance steps. The crowd around me shrieked with joy and broke into applause, and I danced more, I danced backwards until I was up against him, facing away from him, then I leaned into him and took his hands, without looking, and lifted them sideways and moved them with mine in time to the drums, and he danced too, in time with me, and I put a hand behind his neck and pulled his head forward to mine and kissed him, and the crowd roared with delight.

Rome was the first time I had seen him against a white background. At home I had always seen him against black, just as in old films, black and white, quite distinguished, but here it was white on white, and that changed him. When he collected me at the station he was surrounded by other white people, when we walked down the street it was other white people who came towards us, when we ordered coffee it was a white waiter who served us. He was suddenly one of them, one of many, and so was he perhaps the same as them? Back home he had also been one of them, but in a different way: then he was ours, now he was theirs. Did that mean that to find out about him I had to start by finding out about them?

When I had my first menstrual period my mother made me a list of types of men. Since we lived by the sea we were regularly visited by fishing boats and small coastal traders, and the crews were always trying to pick me and my girlfriends up. They're all after one thing, my mother said, all men are, so the question isn't what but how, and she went on to compile a list

79

of men from all over the world, divided into three groups: *Avoid at all costs, Try not to get involved*, and *May be OK*. I always had the list with me, and when ships' crews stopped me to ask the way, as they did all the time, I would take out the list and ask where they came from. Under *Avoid at all costs* deserters from the faith and Eskimos were underlined in heavy ink. 'Are you a deserter or an Eskimo?' I would ask, and they would laugh and try to touch me between the legs. I once bit one of them and he poured with blood and screamed with rage, but I could always run faster than them. Europeans were under *Try not to get involved*, and I remember asking my mother why, and she just said that I would find out if I didn't manage not to get involved, and now it had happened, I had not managed not to get involved with a European, and now I had to find out about them.

'How can I find out about you Europeans?'

We were sitting on a bench by one of the fountains. It seemed quiet all around us, the splashing of the water drowned out the roar of the traffic.

'Watch how we walk. Don't listen to what we say, watch how we walk.'

'And how do Europeans walk?'

'Some walk upwards, some walk downwards, some walk forwards, some walk backwards, some walk to one side, some to the other.'

I tried to follow his advice. When I was visiting him, I tried to notice how people walked, and he was right: it certainly was revealing. Some walked in a way that looked as if they had lost something, others in a way that looked as if they were after something; most walked as if they were trying to hide something, but what could it be? He himself walked differently here, more like them; when he was with us he walked more like us.

Did he have something to hide too?

★

I found a translation of a piece he had written:

'I have never felt at home on big rivers with people dressed in white raising their glasses and laughing. I have always been more intrigued by little tributaries. It has made me someone people only remember fleetingly, someone who was there for a while and then travelled on.'

I liked the image, it was the kind I approved of, with clear lines and plenty of light. But it also made me uneasy. I could see movement in the image, movement out of it. Everything else about the image was clear: the river with its white-painted river-boat, the people on deck, the tall glasses they clinked together; I could hear their laughter, smell the smoke from a fire on the bank, feel the warm breeze. Everything about the image was clear, except at the edges where there was something unclear, someone on the point of leaving.

'Is it you?'

We were standing at a window in his apartment looking at the rain. That was something my mother had taught me, to put everything down when it started raining, to get up when I was woken by rain, because rain is new life, and you should recognize it. At first I was not aware that he did the same, it just felt natural to have him there while I stood watching the rain; but one day the commander slapped us on the shoulder and remarked with a grin that the world's only two rain lovers had found one another, and from then on it was something we did together.

That was at home in my own country, where it doesn't simply rain but cascades straight down like a waterfall for fifteen or twenty minutes. Here it was different, here it might rain hour after hour, day after day. Did he mean us to stand at the window the whole time?

'Is it you?'

Sometimes I had an urge to grab his arm, twist it behind his back, slam him against the wall and hit him hard. I thought it was to make him come out of his vagueness, but it wasn't that. He was at his clearest when he was standing watching the rain.

I could see a 'No' crossing his brow and pushed him against the windowsill.

'Don't lie, just don't lie to me.'

I held him by the front of his shirt and hammered in each word.

'When people write "I" where I come from, they mean it.'

'That's not always the case here.'

We went back to the rain.

'We can't leave till the rain eases up.'

He spoke softly and I could hear an echo of something else in his voice.

'Is this a scene in a film?'

He smiled and put his arm round me. I leaned against him and thought if that was all it was, but it's not. Of course it's him, he was the one who was there for a while and then left; that's how it looks from outside, and now I'm seeing it from inside and what do I see? Do I see someone who observes that it's raining and then leaves, or do I see someone who is waiting for it to stop raining so that he can leave?

He gently dried my cheeks with his fingers, first one side and then the other.

One day I wrote in my notebook:

'Are we as human beings wholly and absolutely responsible for our choices, or are we subject to constraints that deprive us of at least part of the responsibility?

'When I'm with her it's almost never a question, it's only there as brief glimpses, but when I'm away from her, the question persists. And I'm away from her a lot.

'I have problems with her choices in life and find them hard to accept. They make sense, and are logically related, and thus a picture of her character. Is her nature what I have difficulty in accepting?

'Are we as human beings wholly and absolutely responsible for our choices, or are we subject to constraints that deprive us of at least part of the responsibility?

'They say that all's fair in love and war. Is it really? If I put aside all the words of war, put aside the gleam of metal and splinters of steel and torn flesh, if I put aside all these words, a single sentence remains: I am with somebody who has deliberately destroyed the lives of others. And in that sentence I do not hear the sound of love. Will she one day destroy me?'

Will there come a time of loss? Not of longing, but of loss?

I longed for her when I went to the newspaper office in the morning, sat in a departmental meeting, spoke on the telephone; I longed for her when I was having discussions with colleagues, drinking coffee in the canteen, when I locked my door to write; it was an almost physical longing, a yearning, just like being underwater and gasping for air as you reach the surface, that's exactly how it was, my body was gasping for her, to hold her, to hear her voice, to see her smile.

But will there also come a time of loss? I see loss as something completely different from longing; longing is for something you hope is coming, loss is for something you know has gone. Some feel the loss of a time when the children were small; some feel the loss of a place, a house, some the loss of a person, one who has gone away. The time when children were small never returns, and the feeling of loss for a house is usually the loss of the life that the house encapsulated, and that too never returns. We know that we cannot wind life back; that is inherent in our whole experience of time. A person who has gone away never returns, simply exists no more; the picture we had ceases to correspond.

And what is loss? Only a few of the hours of the day are my own, most are set aside for others, but in the few hours that are mine longing can give way to loss, and that sense of loss brings a pain that makes me stop and stand completely still, because then I realize that deep inside me there is someone who knows something. I followed a religion once that tried to wean people away from the sense of loss. It was said that those who do not feel loss are free. And who does not dream of freedom? So I set out on a journey, back to that time.

In Mandalay there stands a little monastery built of teak, ten minutes from the east gate of the old fort. It is constructed in the classic Burmese way, with roofs sloping in all directions and two peristyles. In one of them a group of Buddhist monks sits hunched over the daily text. They are young, some of them still boys: one is playing with a marble, another is dozing off in the suffocating midday heat. Bright burning sunlight streams through the window; an older monk is sitting in a wicker chair. The window has a view over the original part of town, which before the British conquest in 1855 was called 'the Centre of the Universe' and 'the Golden City', but which the British managed to transform within a very short time into a sleepy outpost of their own empire.

The young monk with the marble does not look up when I join him, but responds when I put my hands together to my forehead in greeting. I sit and watch him playing with the marble for a while before speaking to him. He is very skilful, putting a spin on it so that it rolls back to him, even after travelling a metre and a half across the floor.

'If I asked you what the most basic truth in Buddhism was, what would be your answer?'

I speak in a whisper. The peristyle in a Buddhist monastery is not the place for raised voices or lengthy questions.

'That everything and everyone that comes together must sooner or later be parted.'

He rolls the marble towards me as he replies, grey and white, possibly even made of marble rather than glass. It comes to rest in front of me momentarily, rotating on the spot before it turns and rolls back to him.

'And if I asked you what that leads to, what would you answer then?'

'Suffering.'

I sit and watch him playing, making patterns with the marble, making it roll in little circles. It is their economy with words that once made me choose the Buddhist way. No more is said than is strictly necessary. They are not like that in every respect: two blocks from us is what was once called 'the biggest book in the world', seven hundred and twenty-nine marble slabs with the whole of the Buddhist canon engraved on them. It has been calculated that if you read for eight hours a day it would take four hundred and fifty days to read it all. At the fifth Buddhist synod two thousand, four hundred monks read aloud in shifts day and night for almost six months, and some time or another in the course of that time this sentence occurred: 'Everything and everyone that comes together must sooner or later be parted, and until you are able to accept that, you will suffer,' and as I rise I think there must be ways of learning to accept it, if you want to, if you want to. What do you want, do you want to feel loss?

The monk in the wicker chair smiles at me as I sit down. I can see him as little more than a silhouette in the white light from the window. His robe is a deeper red than the robes of the other monks. We sit in silence for a few moments before he asks me, 'What are you seeking?'

'Freedom.'

'From what?'

'Loss.'

We remain sitting in silence. Anywhere else it would have been a long time, but in a monastery time is not measured. He smooths the folds of his robe.

'First go to the Shwedagon Paya, and report the story of the British attempt in 1825 to take the brass bell from the temple built over the strand of the Master's hair: that's a story of the freedom to help oneself. Then go to Mong La and report the story of the five hundred thousand Chinese tourists who cross the border every year: that's a story of the freedom to enjoy oneself. And then come back here.'

Captain Hawthorne is in a bad mood. He has a rash in his groin which is keeping him awake at night, and without enough sleep the days easily turn sour right from the moment you get up. His uniform is too thick, the heat too intense and the natives too numerous. He has tried to bathe the rash with gin and tonic, but it hasn't subsided; he has tried bathing it with ammonia water – oh my God –

'Get those bloody ropes tight now!'

He cracks the whip against his riding boots as he shouts. He has considered going to the regimental doctor but has decided not to; he knows what it is the doctor will tell him to abstain from.

'Captain, the natives won't tighten the ropes. They say there are *nat* in them.'

'*Nat*? Spirits, spirits, spirits! The whole of this bloody country is full of spirits. There are *nat* in the trees, there are *nat* in the water, there are *nat* in the wind, there are *nat* in the stones, there are *nat* in their arses. Tell them there are *nat* in our rifle butts too.'

'Yes, sir.'

He has received a letter from his family, the boys are back at school, his wife has moved from the house in town to the house in the country and she will stay there until the ball season starts. Promotion is two or three months away; with a bit of luck she'll manage to get new visiting cards printed in time.

'Captain, they're still refusing.'

'Beat them.'

He watches the soldiers lay into the Burmese workers, driving them with their rifle butts towards the big bamboo sledge and the plaited sisal ropes. His rash is itching and he is tempted to put his hand in his pocket to scratch, but an officer of Her Majesty's Army does not scratch his private parts in a public place. The workers are screaming, and he can hear the sound of wooden rifle butts against slanting cheekbones, different from the sound of rifle butts against straight cheekbones; his woollen underpants are wet with sweat and clinging to the rash; he could try to loosen them with the hilt of his sword, pretending to straighten it. A Buddhist monk dressed in saffron robes drops to his knees before him with a cry, the Captain turns away, takes a few angry steps to one side, the monk continuing to implore. The Captain beckons over a subordinate.

'Get rid of this ape.'

The soldier kicks the monk in the ribs and yells at him. The Captain walks off to the sledge. The sun is directly overhead, the damned sun, damned heat, damned country. If he leans forward as he walks his pants might ease themselves away from the rash, to some extent at least, rather like when he bows to his wife. Two weeping women try to intercept him, but he goes on, his body at an angle, worrying about the transport problem. The brass bell is fifteen metres high and ten metres in diameter; he guesses it must weigh over twenty tons, and the day is at its hottest. The workers are lying down and sleeping now as usual, damned Burmese, sleeping in the middle of the day. He is not sure whether the sledge will cope with its burden all the way down to the harbour, whether it will manage the weight once in motion. He examines the pagoda again and calls his next-in-command.

'Captain?'

The Lieutenant adopts the same inclined posture as his superior.

'Get it moving.'

'Yes, sir!'

The Lieutenant clicks his heels and salutes, the Captain looks slightly startled. As the Lieutenant stands like that with his heels together and his hand quivering a centimetre from the peak of his cap he gives the impression of having a bad back or being afflicted by some great sorrow, but when he goes over to his subordinates he looks normal: a smart British officer in black uniform at a forty-five-degree angle.

The other officers bend in the same fashion as they take their orders from the Lieutenant, and the marines bend when they in turn receive their orders, and finally the whole company marches off at an angle of forty-five degrees. It is a scene that will be described round camp fires over the whole continent of Asia from generation to generation. Only mad dogs and Englishmen go out in the midday sun, but at least they had enough respect to bow when they took the bell from the Shwedagon Paya.

'Grandad, why did they bow?' 'Shut up and eat your rice, boy.' 'But why did they bow?' 'Because they have *nat* too, however ugly and white they are and however bad they smell; even the British have *nat.*'

At exactly one o'clock the military band strikes up and plays 'Rule Britannia' and a thousand Burmese workers heave on the tow ropes under the British guns, and the sledge creaks and groans and shudders as it begins to move off reluctantly under the weight of the enormous brass bell, slowly and tentatively, as if afraid of the consequences if it is party to abducting the bell from the holy of holies, the Shwedagon Paya, the *chedi* built over eight strands of the Buddha's hair, plucked from his head while he was still alive. When the hairs were placed in a chamber beneath the *chedi* 'there was an uprising of humans and spirits, rays shot from the hairs up into heaven and down into hell, the blind were able to see, the deaf to hear, the dumb to speak, the earth shook, the sea winds raged, the mountains trembled, lightning flashed, precious stones rained down to a depth you had to wade through.' The sledge has heard the workers tell the story so many times that it knows it by heart, word for word, and what can a poor bamboo sledge do against such powers? Nevertheless it sets itself in motion, it dare not resist, a thousand workers are pulling it and a brass band is marching before it and playing so loud that it cannot hear its own *nat,* and behind it walks a group of Buddhist monks with four bounding cats, and you have to be careful of bounding cats. British marines leaning at an angle are positioned on both sides and shouting continuously: the sledge gives up and moves off down towards the river.

Crowds line the route, some weeping, some beating their faces, some just staring wide-eyed. A group of dancers and their shadows come first, the dancers performing one slow dance of mourning, the shadows another, the brass band marching them down the hill in step, as one: 'Rule Britannia'. After the band has passed a voice whispers that they are going to use the bell as a bathtub for their Queen Victoria, and another whispers to ask how big she is to need such a tub, and a man whispers something that makes the women in his vicinity hit him on the head with their parasols; and then the sledge has gone by with its great bell, and the Buddhist monks with their bounding cats, and the spectators follow on at the end of the procession and crane their necks to try to catch a glimpse of the river.

Up ahead the sledge pullers have developed a rhythm and the sledge and its bell gather momentum; the marine escort, still inclined at an angle, almost having to run to keep up. Captain Hawthorne is standing on the jetty beside the barge that is to carry the bell out to a British cargo ship, smiling to himself, assured of a place in history, the man who acquired the Queen's new bathtub; that might be something to have on a visiting card: 'By Appointment, Purveyor of Bathtubs to the Queen'. It took four years to cast the bell, and that ought to be mentioned; he notices that if he bends at a forty-five-degree angle and twists his body to the right, his soaking underpants actually free themselves from the rash, and so that is how he is standing when the brass band comes out on to the jetty and continues playing 'Rule Britannia' on the spot, and that is how he is standing when the first sledge pullers pass the jetty. Pass the jetty? The Captain straightens up and yells 'What the hell do you think you're doing?' and hundreds of smiling sledge pullers pass him on their way out into the river towing the sledge and the bell behind them. The Captain roars 'What the hell is going on?' and the sledge and bell pass the jetty, and the Buddhist monks with the bounding cats pass the jetty and the spectators throng forward in their thousands to see that which will be the climax for those who will relate the story and carry it on from father to son. They will always take a little pause, warm their hands at the camp fire and look teasingly at the wide-eyed children before they go on to tell of the sledge sliding down the river bank and the bell toppling, very slowly, the way twenty tons of metal would topple, and the workers leaping back as it takes in water, and the band playing 'Rule Britannia, Britannia Rules the Waves'. It floats on its side for a few moments before shipping so much water that it begins to sink, like a colossal jug floating with its bottom half submerged, and in the water inside the bell they can see a woman in white bloomers and corset, the Queen, that is how she dresses when she takes a bath, and however sleepy they are the children shout, 'But, Grandpa, Grandpa, if the Captain didn't mean the bell to go out into the river, why did he stand on the jetty looking in the wrong direction?' And the storyteller replies, 'Because he had *nat*, my children.'

Mong La is not significantly different from any other Burmese village. The typical Shan stilt huts are scattered throughout the landscape as they have been for centuries. Over the course of time a Buddhist pagoda and a Christian church have been added, both kept freshly painted: two thin coats covering the Shan people's ancient belief in spirits. The centre is a mix of stone and wooden houses, all in various shades of grey, the colour of poverty.

But Mong La differs from other Burmese villages in one respect: every Saturday the village theatre puts on a production of *Romeo and Juliet*.

My guide gives me back the Burmese notes and waits patiently for me to find Chinese ones. A deep sigh can be heard from behind the box-office window.

We hand our tickets to an usher in a close-fitting white uniform with gold buttons and black riding boots. Our seats are at the back of the stalls, as they are called, but are they called that in a village theatre?

'God knows.'

My guide can sometimes be a little abrupt. The auditorium is elegant, with seats made of teak and imitation leather, the walls burgundy, with chubby pink cherubs painted on them; from the ceiling hangs a chandelier with a massive nebula of matt white plastic stars. There is still half an hour to go before the curtain rises, but the auditorium is already nearly full. I turn to look at the audience, a bad habit of mine.

'Don't stare.'

My guide turns me back round again.

'There aren't many Burmese here?'

'Whisper more quietly.'

I whisper so quietly that she can't hear, 'I'm very lucky to be sitting here with you in a Burmese village, with you and several hundred Chinese men.'

'China is there,' she indicates with a nod of her head.

'There?'

'No, there.'

She smiles and gives me a hug. Someone mutters in the row behind.

The performance begins with three blows on a mighty gong, hauled on to the stage by a man in black leather trousers and a bare torso. He has smeared himself with oil and his muscles gleam every time he lifts the hammer to strike. As he makes his exit, the lights are dimmed and the curtain rises. On a darkened stage stand Romeo and his friends, all dressed in women's clothes: high-heeled shoes, white fishnet tights, flounced tulle skirts and clinging low-cut tops. I whisper, again so softly that neither she nor anyone else can hear, 'I'm so lucky to be sitting here with my guide and several hundred Chinese men in a Burmese village theatre watching Romeo and his friends played by women.'

Romeo has a nasal voice, slightly lisping, and a dreamy look in his eyes. I can't always be sure I'm following the gist of his dialogue, but I think he has already met Juliet; there is something in his manner of speech and bearing that seems to indicate that he has.

'Why is she holding her crotch all the time?'

'He.'

'Why is he holding his crotch all the time?'

'Because he's got an erection.'

'Oh.'

Four stage-hands drag on a scenery-flat representing a balcony, with Juliet standing on it, 'Romeo, Romeo! wherefore art thou Romeo?' There is a sigh from the auditorium. Juliet is wearing tight red leather trousers and a silver lamé waistcoat, her breasts are bare, one pierced, the other not. Behind her stands her chambermaid, played by the man with the gong and the gleaming torso, who has now exchanged his hammer for a long whip. Romeo holds out his arms and calls to her, and a shriek goes up from the audience when he takes his hands away from his crotch. My guide was right. The man with the muscles starts whipping Juliet; she leans over the rail of the balcony and cries out, either in pain or something else, as does the audience.

'Why is he doing that?'

'Because he enjoys it.'

'And what about her?'

'So does she.'

'And Romeo?'

'He does too.'

I am whispering so softly that I can hardly hear it myself. 'I'm so lucky to experience the development of a Burmese village at first hand, after centuries of isolation, at last, half a million Chinese tourists a year just to this border village, this sleepy little border village that has got electricity night and day and a transvestite theatre and a casino and nightclubs and hotels and bars, all staffed by Chinese from top to bottom, and Chinese currency; even the prostitutes are Chinese, imported, you know what you're getting, and there at the end of the four-lane avenue are the sources of finance: a Chinese bank with a marble façade and a brand-new opium museum.'

The men in the auditorium shout after us as we leave. My guide refuses to translate it.

'That wasn't really how I had imagined you would tell the stories.'

'No, I can well believe it.'

The monk is sitting in the same wicker chair, against the same white light, and I have the impression he has been there the whole time I have been up-country. I sit down on the floor at his side.

'Tell me what you have learnt.'

'Becoming attached to things is to expose yourself to suffering, because things are always taken away from you; becoming attached to people is to expose yourself to suffering, because people always leave.'

'Mong La is about becoming attached to people?'

'Mong La is about sexuality; next to violence the strongest attachment of one person to another.'

He turns and looks at me, just for a second.

'And what conclusion do you draw from that?'

'If you manage to overcome the desire to own things, you are free; if you manage to overcome the desire to become attached to other people, you are free.'

He nods.

'And what is the way?'

I hesitate before replying, and I can hear as I speak that the words are coming unwillingly, as if they had no desire to be spoken.

'Meditation. Until the mind becomes like a smooth shining forest lake where people and things are reflected without ever breaking the surface.'

I close my eyes and can see her standing by the water in uniform; she puts down her rifle, takes off her clothes and plunges in, breaking the surface and diving deeper. I am out there in the water and see her dive, see her swimming towards me underwater, smiling, her hair streaming behind her and her face slightly distorted by the refraction of light in the water. She comes up just in front of me and pushes her hair back and laughs, puts her arms round me and holds me tight. I laugh and yell as she ducks us both under.

'Was that what made you leave Buddhism?'

I nod.

'You are not Asiatic.'

I feel calm inside. I understand what he means. Asia always depresses me; nowhere else does the human condition stare me more brutally in the face.

'What is the worst?'

I turn towards him to see the answer, not just hear it; I squint towards the white light and can just make out that his eyes are focused on something distant.

'This damned rice. I have eaten rice every single day since I was born, and I will eat rice every single day until I die. After death I shall be reincarnated into a new life of rice. I know someone who has been reincarnated thirteen times. If you reckon that life is a bowl of rice every day for seventy years and multiply the sum by thirteen, it makes three hundred and thirty-two thousand, one hundred and fifty bowls of rice. That's a devil of a lot of rice.'

It is the longest speech I have heard him make.

He turns towards me.

'What sort of picture do you Europeans have of freedom?'

'We have two. One of freedom as a matter of chance, and one of freedom as the opposite. Which do you think is correct?'

He stands up, takes off his sandals, places them on his head and leaves.

IMMORTALITY

I think the physical bond between us became increasingly obvious after the war was over and we spent more time together. When we were with friends we always sat apart and made a point of circulating, as was the custom in my country, a custom we also followed when we were in his. But even when we were at opposite ends of the room I could feel a chemistry between us.

We displayed our mutual feelings less when we were in the company of others in my country, partly because that was how things were done there and partly because a relationship with a person of his race was still felt by many as a provocation. When I was with him in Europe, we didn't need to be so restrained; then I might suddenly come up behind him while he was engaged in conversation and put my arms around him and he would go on talking with a smile in his eyes. Sometimes he might equally suddenly pick me up, put me over his shoulder and walk off while I pummelled his back shrieking with laughter.

But the best image I have of us is quite different, and indicative of something more than either love or friendship. It is of us in my country, in the evening, walking along a narrow street on both sides of which were fires in front of little stalls, and the air was full of the aroma of grilled maize and roasting bananas. The way we walked must have said something about us, people who saw us nodded. We stopped and bought some roasted nuts, exchanged a few words with the woman selling them, took our leave and went on, found a table in a café and ordered. We scarcely spoke to each other, but I think we both communicated with our surroundings, with the darkness, with the smells and the distant music; communicating I believe as one, absorbing the same impressions.

He gradually changed in a way that took me a long time to see and even longer to admit to myself. It was hardly noticeable and then only in little things, small details that took me by surprise, made me stop and think. If I had sat down and added all the details together, I would have seen the change; I don't know whether I would have tried to do anything about it, whether I would have wanted to or been able to, but I would have seen it.

When I wrote the sign of our covenant on his forehead with blood and poison, there was light in his eyes, clear, calm light when he agreed to it. When we went to bed later on I could feel his gratitude really close to me, not just in my body but in all of me, my thoughts, my feelings, my dreams. We used to dream together. He asked me to open the dream, carefully, and I opened it the way a child opens a box of treasures, slowly, in anticipation. I used to point to the first image, men in black trousers and white shirts running across a green field, two eyes rising from a lake beside a town. He used to acknowledge the image and then roll over and go to sleep.

That's how it was, and that's how it is, but something has changed. At first I would often hear him whisper something just as he was going to sleep, a few words as he was slipping away, a few words that would hover in the darkness above us, as if he were trying to hold on. I used to lay my hand on his arm until the night had taken him, my other hand covering the words suspended above us.

All that has changed. He no longer whispers when the

night comes to fetch him; it's as if something in him has burnt itself out. When the light brings him back the next morning, he needs less time to wake up.

Something else has changed. When I make the sign of our pact on his forehead, there is still light in his eyes, but there is something else there too. I asked him to tell me all the words he associated with 'gratitude', since he lives by words, and from his response I reached out and plucked the word 'fondness'. Fondness, that is what has come into his eyes. It might be because I no longer make the sign of our pact on his forehead every night, but I don't think so, I think it's something else. I washed his trousers one evening without asking, which he doesn't like; he doesn't want other people washing his clothes, but now he is here and that is what we do. I found four teeth in one of the pockets, from a sheep or a goat, and I didn't like it; I held them in my hand and I didn't like it; I wished I had found something that was more normal in men's pockets, a revolver, a rosary, a keyring with a naked brass lady on it, or some kif. Yet here I stood holding four teeth and didn't like it.

'When did you start hammering teeth into acacia trees?'

He had just come in, and stood in the doorway with a surprised look on his face.

'At Easter.'

'Didn't you know that's something we're trying to stop people doing?'

'Yes. You'll soon have cut down every single acacia tree in the whole town; it's hard not to be aware of it.'

'Can you please stop saying "you"?'

'Then you'll have to stop saying "we".'

I don't know which hurt most, realizing that I thought 'them' and 'us', or realizing that he was on his way over to 'them'. I tried to revert to the subject unemotionally as we ate.

'How can development be brought about in a country

where people think they can influence their lives by hammering animal teeth into tree trunks?'

'I'm not trying to bring about development anywhere.'

'Come off it. Do you think we spent all our youth at the front only for people to go on with forced marriages and dowries and polygamy and the suppression of women and circumcision and magic?'

'I'm sorry. I didn't mean that.'

'It's all right.'

And so I didn't have to ask whether it was in solidarity with the people that you had taken up magic, and you didn't have to say yes and know that it was only part of the truth.

———————

She gradually changed. I can say to the exact second when I noticed it, and then as I looked back over our time together I could see all the portents I had not been aware of. I know that parts of myself must have recognized changes along the way and reacted to them, because recognition is both deeper and slower than conscious reflection, but I know too that the change came out of the blue. There is no contradiction in that, just a paradox, the paradox inherent in human beings.

I usually read to her or tell her stories when we sit together in the evenings. It's quiet around us then, wherever we are, and I always have the feeling of a new beginning. If I read a piece I have written myself, she tends to put her hand on my arm, close but not too close, because I feel vulnerable when I read my own work, and she knows that. If I read a piece others have written, she usually leans back to look at me, following me and the words with her eyes. And if I tell her a story, she leans forward in eager anticipation.

That's how it has been and how it is, but there is a distinct change. One evening she asked me to tell her something unusual or remarkable, as she occasionally does, and I told her about the ark of the covenant. My paper wanted me to write a piece on the legend that it was kept in this part of the world, not far from her country, and I had enjoyed the research.

'Ark of the covenant?'

'The ark of the covenant. The box that was constructed for the two stone tablets that Moses received from God, the very foundation stone of both your religion and that of the Jews and Christians.'

'What's so remarkable about that?'

'It could move on its own. "And they departed from the mount of the Lord three days' journey: and the ark of the covenant of the Lord went before them in the three days' journey, to search out a resting place for them. And it came to pass, when the ark set forward, that Moses said, 'Rise up, Lord, and let thine enemies be scattered; and let them that hate thee flee before thee.' And when it rested, he said, 'Return, O Lord, unto the many thousands of Israel.'" Numbers, 10, 33–36.'

'What's so remarkable about that? A box that can move? Is that all?'

I smiled. In her world boxes could move. But there was something in her eyes that I could not quite fathom.

'The ark emitted such a powerful light that Aaron's two sons Nadab and Abihu both died when they attempted to approach it. Even Moses' face was burnt and he had to wear a veil for the rest of his life.'

'So as not to get any more sun on his skin?'

'Because his face radiated nearly as much light as the ark. The ark was always packed in thick coverings when they were transporting it in order not to harm the bearers.'

'I thought you said it could move by itself?'

'That's exactly what has always puzzled me.'

She came closer.

103

'Can we try and get this straight? It can move, it has to be carried, it gives off so much light that people get burnt by it and die, but not so much that it can't be contained by a few covers. What happened next?'

'That's what is so remarkable. The ark disappeared and was hardly mentioned again. We are talking of the holiest relic that ever existed in Mosaic culture, it emitted fire and light, burnt those who went near it, stopped the flow of rivers, demolished mountains, annihilated whole armies and destroyed cities. The Bible alone mentions the ark of the covenant more than two hundred times up to the reign of King Solomon, and then suddenly goes completely silent on the subject. Not so much as "one day the ark had gone" or "no one knew what became of it"; nothing – just a deafening silence. Solomon built a temple for the ark, but after his time, three thousand years ago, the ark of the covenant simply ceased to exist.'

She sat back with a detached look in her eyes. When I think of it, that look was the first sign I noticed, and I should have understood it.

'Perhaps it was stolen?'

I could hear a noise now, of thundering hooves, a herd rushing towards me at full gallop.

'And carried off in the middle of the night by thieves in dark clothes sneaking out of the city gate? Thieves who waited for a moment when the guards were looking the other way so that they wouldn't see the sparks and flames from the ark and hear its roar?'

She contemplated her nails, picking at one of them.

'Perhaps the stone tablets were two meteorites that went on glowing for a while after they fell and were then elaborated in the popular imagination? I've read that Semitic tribes at the time used to imbue meteorites with religious significance because they came from the skies, from heaven. The Black Stone of Mecca is an example.'

An abyss opened beneath me and I could hear shouts from far below, and I realized that the herd galloping towards me at breakneck speed was my own heart. I turned my head and listened to the sound of her words, the harsh metallic sound of logic, no longer the soft sound of magic.

———————————

We never talked about marriage. Maybe we knew it might provoke something more, a cultural choice, and we felt ourselves still in transition, each leaving one culture for another.

On the other hand we talked of the future, of moments we wanted to last. But for the most part it was my future we talked of, my work, in my capital city, and his presence there. His future was almost never contemplated, and if it was, we spoke only of a few months hence.

We would occasionally exchange thoughts about a time beyond those few months, but without using words. That was when he travelled directly back from the killing fields to me, paler and more silent than usual. Then I would look at him and say nothing, just following him with my eyes: down the aircraft steps, into the baggage hall, through customs, holding him away from me to see him better, not taking my eyes off him even in the car into town, on the stairs up to the apartment. Something passed between us then about the future, his future, and before I drew the curtains and closed the future out I would always stand for a moment to watch the life on the street below.

Where was his reporting taking him? My Italian was getting better and as time went on I was gradually finding myself able to read most of what he wrote. I remember one piece in particular, when he had managed to get inside a town under siege:

'The plane carrying aid comes in over the besieged town at a great height and banks steeply down towards the airport in a vertiginous corkscrew manoeuvre that makes it a harder target for anti-aircraft fire.

'I am lying on top of a pallet of maize sacks, hanging on to the net that covers them and waiting. There are no windows in the hold.

'The plane comes out of its spiral into a long slow curve, straightens up suddenly and bumps down on to the runway. I stay where I am on the pile of maize until the plane has come to a complete stop.

'The cargo doors open, armed soldiers jump in, yelling at my camera. Out on the runway fifty or so young boys are running around the plane with empty tin cans in their hands, hoping for a sack to break during the unloading.

'The soldiers hit out at them, the boys run off shrieking, turn and come back towards the plane again.

'The airport is like a fortress; armoured cars, artillery, soldiers with automatic weapons and mute expressions. The road into town is lined by thousands of people, sitting shoulder to shoulder. If food is coming into town, it has to come this way.

'The town has been kept under siege by rebel forces for a year and a half, surrounded by two rings of steel: one of mines, one of machine guns. Anyone trying to get out is killed – blown up or shot.

'The garrison of government troops cut off in the town is demoralized, not strong enough to break out and not getting enough supplies in to build up its strength. The garrison takes out its frustration on the civilian population.

'The town was built for two hundred and fifty thousand people, and is now housing four hundred thousand. In the last few weeks before the siege there were tens of thousands streaming in every single day, in from the front, away from the front. The whole infrastructure has collapsed, sewage is running through the open streets, epidemics spread with the water, electricity has been cut off.

'A heavy, sickly-sweet odour hangs over the town. In the gardens in front of shelled houses there are rows of newly dug graves. In the humid heat, crowds of people wander the streets of the centre, most of them with the blank faces of the shell-shocked.

'In the market there are some women trying to sell vegetables. At a long table a group of government soldiers is getting drunk; they have money to pay with, goods to barter with.

'"Every single time we get a planeload of food in, the soldiers come and help themselves," an aid worker sighs. "We have no means of stopping them; neither their officers nor the police will intervene."

'At a food-distribution centre a cluster of children-pressing tearfully up against the gates is driven away by adult guards. Inside there are rows of children eating a meal of rice from tin plates. They eat soundlessly, without looking up from the food.

'A twelve-year-old boy stops me, his whole family has died of famine, he is the last one left, do I have any food?

'In front of a Catholic mission station a young girl stands in a red dress, her upper arms the thickness of a finger, the bones rubbing against the red cloth of her dress.

'Everything in the town is closed, everything in the town is shot to pieces, everything in the town has been plundered. Only the army is functioning, aggressive soldiers in camouflage uniform and decrepit jeeps following every move I make.

'I climb aboard the empty cargo plane and lie down on the floor with my feet up against one of the empty pallets. The hatch is closed and the last thing I see is children's hands scraping up flour off the runway with their fingernails. One sack tore. I am sure that if I close my eyes I will hear the sound of little nails against asphalt above the roar of the engines. But I don't shut my eyes, not yet, I have to find something to hang on to before the plane takes off.'

I stopped reading, I could hear his silent scream: How can a rebel movement ever contemplate blockading four hundred thousand people and letting them die of hunger? How can the world ever contemplate inviting such a rebel movement to the negotiating table?

Where was his reporting taking him? Should I try to stop him?

———————————

One evening she told me something. She told me with her eyes when she got off the bus and saw me on the balcony, she told me with her footsteps up the stairs, she told me in the way she came through the door, she told me in the face she laid against my shoulder; my shoulder, not chest or cheek as she usually did. I held her and heard the stream of life in me in full flood, the close weave of feelings that can only be grasped intuitively, and for a few seconds everything was possible, right up to the moment when she raised her head to meet my eyes and tell me.

'No!'

My scream hit the wall with enough impact to make it shake; she covered her face with her hands in fear. I screamed again, the scream welling up from below, tearing upwards and outwards right through me. I leapt up and ran to the wall, skidded and crashed into it and felt the pain of torn flesh. Her big brown eyes were fixed upon me, anxious and sad.

I crouched down in front of her and shouted, 'It can't be true!'

I shouted it over and over again, desperately trying to hold her gaze, like a drunkard struggling to find something to clutch at, in no condition to believe there isn't anything. She took my head in her arms and held it to her lap, as if to console me, to say goodbye; I lay with my eyes open, seeing nothing. Time stopped, the room stood still, and everything fused into a great block of granite. The real became unreal and the unreal real. There was no longer any before or after, and what she had said might or might not be inside the granite block.

I could still see nothing when she carefully lifted my head and stood up. It was not my head she laid back on the seat of the chair but something else, and the sound of the door closing as she went out was not just a sound but a melody, a melody that gradually filled me until it had displaced every-thing else.

Never again. The two most unendurable words a person can hear, and the basis of all religion. Never again: we cannot live with the certain knowledge of never again, we have to find a way round the two words, a faith, a myth that there will always be an again.

Never again. I stood up slowly and unsteadily. Never again. She came from a part of the world where people are not careless with words, and I myself had increasingly lost my faith in words. Never again: she had used only a few words and a few seconds to tell me, and my scream had prolonged the words and the seconds, not by much, just a little way into eternity, and now that I was back on my feet, time and the room enclosed me again, and it was after she had said it; the time before she had said it was gone for ever.

I went over to the window and watched her cross the courtyard and turn and wave before disappearing into the archway and out into reality on the other side, the reality in which I was simply a visitor, now more than ever.

I went down the stairs and out of reality, out of one and into another. The aroma of spices drew me towards it, and the sound of sand, and colours. An aged face smiled at me, from a doorway came music and light, a man and a woman were dancing in a room, the woman leaning her head back as she danced, studying him, enjoying him. I walked on, a beggar held out his hands to me and spoke and I bent down and put a coin in them, bent right over, rolled myself round, stood up and went on, roll life round, an old Burmese expression, roll round life; behind me I could hear her calling, but faintly, as if she were uncertain, or too distant. Had I already moved so far, a whole reality away?

I went towards the beat of drums beyond the marketplace. The sun was setting and the world consisted of shadows, bigger than the houses and people that cast them. Shadow-land, shadowland. If we could gather the shadows together and take them with us everything would be simpler: we would have only one reality, not two. And then suddenly the shadows were gone, together with her voice, and a woman recognized me and stopped me, grabbed me by the shoulder, looked me in the eyes and said it had all gone wrong, none of them had come back, those who had come back were so changed that it was not them. I shook her off me and asked how she had recognized them then, and I could hear that I was shouting, in anger, in desperation, how did you recognize them, and she shrank back, lowered her eyes. I walked on. When the journey is the goal, all people become transient, all of them, every single one.

A warm, dark night and the sound of a voice, rising upwards with the smells and sounds from the street below, finding the sheet I had wrapped around myself and insinuating itself, between my face and the pillow, touching my hand that I had pushed under the pillow.

'You must draw up a pact with her.'

'We have one already.'

I spoke into the pillow, it muffled the words, muted them.

'Another one. The original covenant between God and man. If you do as I say, then.'

'Then what?'

'What do you want? Not to lose her?'

'Will I lose her?'

'What did she say to you this afternoon?'

I bit into the pillow to restrain myself.

'What did she say to you this afternoon?'

I shut my eyes and buried my face in the pillow. It made me feel invisible.

'You dare not put it into words, because you think words solidify things. Did she say that she was ill, that she was dying, or that she was leaving you?'

'What does it matter? The result is the same.'

'Are you that devastated?'

I turned on my side, covered my mouth and nose with my hands and sobbed.

The voice had gone, leaving only the warmth and the darkness and the sounds from the street. I wanted to reach behind me to feel whether she was lying there, whether she might have been the one who had whispered, not just a voice inside myself, but I was afraid to. First to Axum, the Ethiopians' holy capital where the ark of the covenant is said to be preserved. Then reach out for her again and ask whether it was indeed she who had whispered.

Axum approaching the end of its second millennium, a noisy toiling city of corrugated iron and tea huts and muddy backstreets; flocks of goats and chickens and car horns, cafés full of boisterous soldiers and tables laden with beer bottles and sullen waitresses in slippers. Axum approaching the end of its second millennium, a city so completely anchored in the present that it would be hard to imagine it had a past, let alone a future, had it not been for the statues in the park on the edge of town and near the Royal Palace: silent granite witnesses to its Golden Age in the first five hundred years of our time-reckoning, when the city was a destination for the Arabs and Romans and Greeks and the Nubians with their caravans, and was a world centre, a focal point in a world that was different, that had a different view of itself.

Even Saint Mary of Zion had a forgotten air, a modest little brick church with high narrow windows and a small cupola and a white picket fence. The priest who unlocked the door wore a black robe and black hat and had very, very ancient skin.

'They say the ark of the covenant is kept here?'

'That's right.'

Of course it is. Where else would the holy of holies of Christianity be kept, except here on a parched plateau of brick houses and burning sun?

'The ark of the covenant?'

'That's right.'

A sudden roll of drums in the background, and four hundred trumpets sounded a fanfare.

'The ark with the two stone tablets?'

'Do I get the impression you're finding this hard to believe?'

The priest examined my face closely. He had a plaited red cord around his waist and a white beard. The church wall behind him was grey and partly covered in green lichen. He gestured towards a broken half-open door.

'Through that door, down two flights of steps, straight on, turn left after the condom machine.'

'Condom machine?'

'Yes. Condom machine.'

'A condom machine outside the room containing the ark of the covenant?'

'Symbolic. The Queen of Sheba became pregnant when she visited King Solomon in Jerusalem. She gave birth immediately after she returned. The condom machine is a reminder never to go on a journey without condoms.'

'Her son, Menelik?'

'He travelled to visit his father in Jerusalem when he was twenty. He was received like a prince. That created envy. In the end the Council of Elders demanded that the son should be sent back here. King Solomon agreed, but imposed the condition that all the Elders should send their first-born sons to accompany him. Among them was Azarius, son of Zadok, the high priest. He was the one who stole the ark of the covenant and brought it with him.'

I closed my eyes and let everything slide into place. I knew that the once legendary emperor of this country had called himself the 255th descendant of Menelik, son of the Queen of Sheba, but the question of Menelik's father had always been shrouded in mystery. A queen obviously has the right to keep certain things to herself. I knew too that there were the remnants of a Jewish tribe in this country, the Falashas, or black Jews, who practised an archaic form of Judaism and dreamt of returning to Israel. They were airlifted to Israel when Israel was experiencing a falling population in the eighties. Now I knew who had founded the tribe.

'Are you the custodian of the ark?'

'Yes.'

'May I see it?'

'No, I'm sorry. I'm the only one who has permission to go near it. It used to be exhibited at special religious festivals, but it was always wrapped up in thick covers. To protect people.'

'Against what?'

'Its power. Do you see that obelisk over there? It's reckoned to be the biggest monolith of antiquity, thirty-five metres high and five hundred tons in weight. It was the ark of the covenant that raised it.'

I shaded my eyes as I scrutinized the obelisk and tried to work out for myself how the ark might have raised it. Parts of it were now lying in pieces on the ground, but it was historically documented that it had stood for hundreds of years, so somehow it must have been raised into position, with or without the ark. If every worker could lift a hundred kilos, they would have needed five thousand workers to erect it, which would have been a physical impossibility, since they would not all have been able to get round it. I suddenly felt dizzy and put my hand on the priest's shoulder. He took one look at me and led me over to a stone seat, sat me down and sat himself next to me.

'That's a normal reaction. Just rest for a few minutes.'

'I don't belong to your religion, but can I make confession to you anyway?'

'That is quite usual too. Go ahead.'

He took out a pink plastic electronic game and pressed some buttons. There was a little whine and three short beeps in quick succession, then more rhythmical noises as he obviously began playing something to and fro. I began with what she had told me and then wound time back, to our days together and apart, to her village, the final assault, and the front; I wound time further back to her schooldays and my studies, I rewound until I was standing with my forehead against that of a Tibetan monk, felt a transmission of power, and was admitted.

'Have you told me everything?'

He stopped playing.

'I've left out the killing fields.'

'Why?'

'Because I can't bring myself to talk about them.'

He looked down at the game, as if not sure whether to resume. Then he asked, as if as an afterthought, 'When the Tibetans took you in, did they make any demands on you?'

'Yes. To stop doing everything that was harmful to me.'

'Have you managed that?'

'No.'

The priest turned his attention to his game again and I closed my eyes. The sun was warm on my face. The short electronic whizz emitted every time he presumably killed an enemy made all other sounds seem unreal; the goats in the little wood next to the churchyard and the women beating their wet washing down at the river belonged to another reality, far away. Our reality was different, it was a struggle to climb to the next level, and my life lay in the priest's hands.

'What does the word "loss" mean in your language?'

He didn't look up as he spoke. I could hear that the battle was nearing a climax, the whizzing sounds were coming fast and furious.

'Harm.'

'Why harm?'

'Because we have lost something.'

'Something you had?'

'Yes.'

'How have you lost it?'

'It has been taken from us.'

'Only that?'

'Or we have renounced it.'

He went on playing for a while in silence.

'Do you feel better now?'

He still didn't look up.

'A bit.'

He began to go red in the face and pant for breath. The

whizzes from the game were coming in waves, and between each whizz there was an explosion. The priest could hardly sit still, his hands shook and he lurched forward at each press of the button. Suddenly the game gave a screech followed by an unsyncopated electronic tune and the priest raised it to his lips and kissed it. Then he turned and addressed me to my face.

'You must carry on writing about dreams, for your sake, for her sake, for the sake of your love. That was what she told you. Why is it so difficult?'

'I can't manage it.'

'You can't or you don't want to?'

I didn't respond.

He leaned towards me. 'You started so appropriately, with oblivion. Our dreams lie on the other side of that. Dreams are the bridge that transports us over the abyss of oblivion.

'Just as faith is the bridge that transports us over the abyss of doubt.'

He smiled and nodded.

Later that day I sat in a pavement café trying to keep my balance on another bridge, the bridge between dreams and myths. I held my arms out to steady myself; the sun was low and I could see the shadows of my outstretched arms and the shadow of the waitress who put her hand on one of them.

'Are you OK, mister?'

'More or less. How about you?'

'Same here. Would you like another beer?'

'If you can bring it without falling off.'

'Off what?'

'The bridge between dreams and myths. It's right there.' I pointed.

'I wouldn't dream of it.'

She came back with another bottle, smiled and went again. She was young, in her twenties, elegant.

I turned the beer mat over and wrote:

'What are dreams? I think there are little cracks in human consciousness, little cracks that dreams seep through. I see us being drawn towards these cracks, like moths to a flame, because we have no choice. We give form to what seeps in through these cracks with our language of symbols. But what lies behind these cracks, behind human consciousness? I think that is where myths are to be found, the archetypal in us, that which both precedes and is yet independent of the culture we happen to find ourselves in. If it were possible to crawl through these cracks and out the other side we would find something common to all human beings, a landscape of specifically human longings, a tranquil valley with a broad river flowing through it.'

The waitress came back, saw what I had written, lifted my bottle to see if it was empty, and gave me an enquiring glance. I nodded. When she brought the next one she also had a new pile of beer mats.

'You look as if you need to write for a while.'

I thanked her, picked one up and began writing.

'What are myths? It is just on two hundred and seventy-five years ago that Giambattista Vico wrote that myths are human beings' attempt to solve the riddles of life and the universe, an attempt to find connections in the unconnected, explanations of the inexplicable. Carl Gustav Jung added that myths are more than that, they embody the archetypes that have such a profound effect on the human psyche. Bronoslaw Malinowski showed from his fieldwork in the Trobriand Islands that myths are also used to give legitimacy to social stratification. And Claude Lévi-Strauss charted the way myths are used to reconcile what we experience as contradictions in life: either very concrete ones, such as that between life and death, or the extremely abstract, such as that between unity and multiplicity, one of the first philosophical questions ever posed in our culture.'

The waitress stood behind me watching as I wrote, her hand resting lightly on my shoulder. She probably knew the Roman alphabet and was waiting for words she recognized. She leaned over and pointed at Lévi-Strauss.

'Is that the Levi's trousers man?'

'Yes.'

I saw our shadows merge. For a moment both her hands were on my shoulders.

'I like 501s best. Then I can feel that I'm moving. Another beer?'

She held up the empty bottle and I nodded again. When she came back I had filled another beer mat. She took it from me. 'Lévi-Strauss, again?'

'Yes.'

'What are you writing about him?'

I took back the beer mat and translated:

'Lévi-Strauss was the one who had the most comprehensive material; he collected and interpreted more than eight hundred myths and was the first to document the fact that myths give rise to as many questions as they answer, and that those questions are taken up by other myths, in other places, at other times.'

When I had finished she took the beer mat, put it in the back pocket of her jeans and said, 'The same thought has struck me.'

———

'The Somme?'

'In France.'

The Somme was one of the first places in Europe he showed me. We travelled by train, and I stood for hours at the window in the corridor observing the landscape. After the plains of Italy, the Swiss Alps, then German fields and French vineyards. I kept calling to him in the compartment and pointing things out; there was always something in the landscape that caught my attention, an irrigation system, a dam, an artificial dyke.

Just before I went to sleep on the first night I said into the darkness, 'Are you allowed to change the natural landscape so much?'

In Amiens we hired a tandem to continue our journey; he said it was important to arrive as quietly as possible. I had no experience of cycles, so it took us an unsteady hundred metres and a couple of falls before I acquired the knack. We stopped in a village to buy food, lemonade, wine, glasses, plates and a blue check tablecloth. I noticed that the people serving us seemed to have no problem understanding his French, and I held his hand proudly. The Germans had seemed rather less enthusiastic.

We cycled on through the rolling green countryside. He had waved at the horizon and told me that the sea was over there, and I imagined the fields around us as great heavy swells of ocean that had rolled in over the land and turned green, here and there sprouting into little groves of trees.

There were trees growing along both verges, and beyond them occasional glimpses of houses, small houses with white walls and red roofs. Gradually the distances between them increased until finally there were none. We came to a halt by tacit consent, leaned the bicycle against a tree, walked a few metres off the road and sat down on the lush green grass. He spread out the blue check cloth and laid it with glasses and plates; I unpacked the food: salad, paté and bread. Neither of us said anything until I had drunk some lemonade and he some wine. Then he looked at me.

'If you ever feel the urge to study European cultural history, you should start here. You can go back later to the Renaissance and the Enlightenment, or forward to what's called modern times, but you should begin here. The key to European culture is to be found here.'

I gazed over his shoulder at the rows of white crosses on a green background a kilometre wide extending as far as the eye could see.

'How many?'

'Two million. A million in the battle of 1916 and a million in the battle of 1917.'

'Who won?'

'Neither side.'

'What did they achieve?'

'Nothing.'

We ate in silence, and a long way off we could see someone putting flowers by one of the crosses.

'But they died for something?'

'We have to hope so.'

We went on eating, he drank some wine, read the label, and I leaned forward and tried to read it with him. Behind us the sun suddenly broke through and shone on the endless rows of white crosses.

'Is it better to die if you die for a cause?'

He was the one asking the question.

'Certainly not for the one who dies. But maybe for those who are left.'

We were speaking in hushed tones, as if we didn't want to disturb the crosses in the cemetery. He lay on one elbow looking up at me.

'When the first written language was developed by the Sumerians five thousand years ago, what do you think was the first thing they wrote?'

'Would anyone care to correspond with us?'

I ducked as he pretended to aim a blow at me and laughed.

'What did they write, then?'

'About death.'

He inclined his head towards the white crosses.
I started packing up our things.
'When are you leaving?'

———————

Babylon is like suburbs everywhere, a little indetermi-
nate, hardly visible from the bus. The driver has to get
the couple in front of me to tug at my shirt before he can
catch my attention and point.

'Al Mahrouk.'

'Babylon?'

He nods.

'Many thanks. When is there a bus back?'

'Tomorrow. If we're not bombed.'

I swing my rucksack over my left shoulder and get off.
The whole of me is in that movement, all my thoughts
and feelings, and certainly all my longings. Rucksack over
the left shoulder and off, a bus, a train, a ferry.

I pause for a moment and look about me. I have been
dropped on a little square with streets radiating out in
the form of a star. In one is a post office and a barber's, in
another stalls selling mineral water and tea, in a third
food shops and a kebab hut. I close my eyes and smile,
knowing that something completely different will happen to me if I go down one street rather than another,
and I sometimes wonder whether that is what attracts
me most about travelling, always being able to choose
my own future.

I select the street with the food shops and the kebab
hut, not for any special reason, that is just how it goes.
One food shop sells canned food and vegetables, sar-
dines from the Arab Emirates, Indian spinach in water,
fresh pumpkins and onions. The other sells meat and

fish, freshly slaughtered sheep and chickens under a dense cloud of flies, and dried perch from the Nile.

'Salad and dressing?'

The man in the kebab hut is in his late fifties, heavily built, with greying, curly hair and a moustache that makes the corners of his mouth droop.

'Yes, please.'

'American?'

'European.'

'Weapons inspector?'

'No.'

'Chilli?'

'Yes, please.'

I put my rucksack down against the wall and my elbow on the counter. The food shop is across the street, directly opposite, and from time to time a customer goes in or out, usually a well-nourished woman. The air is still, the heat in the atmosphere seems to compress it and amplify the noise of cars, the prayer calls from the minaret, the buzz of flies around the meathooks.

'Do you think there have always been flies? Or are they a recent phenomenon?'

'Hard to say.'

'Capers?'

'Yes, please.'

'A friend of mine read that the flies are sent by the Israelis.'

'That wouldn't surprise me.'

'What brings you here?'

'The Tower of Babel.'

'The Tower of Babel?'

He leans out of the hut with the assurance that comes with middle age and points: 'Down there. On the overgrown piece of land with the white board.'

My eyes follow his gesture towards the place where the world began. A wilderness of a plot with a crumbling wall and a rusty sign.

'Why the Tower of Babel?'

'Someone I know wants to see it.'

'Marinated goat or smoked perch?'

'Smoked perch.'

'It must have been hell to have been the foreman there. One day everyone speaking the same language, the next day no one, and nobody understanding anyone else. How could they have given out instructions?'

'Would have been difficult.'

'It would have given me a headache. Just for the sake of a silly notion, to build a tower up to heaven. The gods could have inflicted bubonic plague or scabies or something on them, but instead they made them all start speaking separate languages.'

He throws up his hands.

'Ah, well. God is God and man is man, and that's how it's meant to be.'

Is it? Here I stand at the beginning of the world, at the very first question: Why did the gods make us mortal and themselves immortal? It was five thousand years ago, long before Christianity made it forbidden to ask. At that time inquisitiveness was not considered a sin, and human beings demanded to know. They built a tower to heaven to confront the gods. Why have you made us mortal and yourselves immortal? And from the top of the tower they shot an arrow straight up, and when it came down again covered in blood they applauded triumphantly. Look, they're like us after all! But their triumph was short-lived, because people still went on dying and the gods went on living, and the gods punished mankind by giving them different languages so that they could no longer understand one another. For that very reason the story has come down to us in many different languages. The Sumerian, Akkadian and Babylonian texts are the best preserved, and it was turned into a myth, the myth of Gilgamesh, the king who was two-thirds man and one-third god, the despot whom the gods tried to tame by creating Enkidu, the wild man covered in hair who lived with wild beasts until he slept with a prostitute and became civilized. Gilgamesh and Enkidu became friends and Enkidu undertook to explore the kingom of the dead for Gilgamesh, but failed to return. Just his shadow slipped out through a hole that the god Enki had made in the ground; but that was sufficient: the shadow told Gilgamesh how bad things were in the kingdom of death. Gilgamesh crossed the waters of death and found the plant of immortality at the bottom of the sea, only to have it stolen from him by a serpent. In the end the tragic moral: death is inevitable and all hope of immortality is vain.

The Tower of Babel slowly collapsed, and the site became a derelict plot of ground in an Iraqi suburb, bombed with surgical precision. How courageous they must have been, how unafraid. They dared the unthinkable, to challenge the gods, by building a tower up to heaven; and then they accepted their defeat and formed it into a myth, the first in the world, so that everyone could share it: we are mortal, and all hope of anything else is vain.

'Have you been here before?'

The man in the hut is leaning over the counter towards me.

'Yes.'

'Will you be coming again?'

I nod.

'May I offer you a cup of tea?'

He motions with his head towards the back door of the hut. The house is built round an open courtyard, in the middle of which is a fountain, the figure of a little boy holding a fish with a jet of water spurting from its mouth. In front of the fountain is a stone seat. He sits down and, patting his hand on the bench, invites me to do the same.

We sit in silence for a while.

'Lovely house? It used to be lovelier. As we all were.'

His wife crosses the courtyard with a basket of washing, smiles at me without meeting my gaze; there is a flash of gold teeth. He follows her with his eyes until she is out of view, and then sighs.

'A man will endure much for thirty date palms, but what about when enduring isn't enough?'

'Then it can be difficult.'

His wife reappears, her basket empty; another glint of gold. She is broad and buxom. He waits until she has gone and then says, 'Sometimes I imagine others, and then it's fine, but once I got into trouble for whispering the name of the one I was thinking of, and then it wasn't.'

'I can believe that.'

'Because of the trade boycott it's hard to get imported goods, even on the black market, and this hasn't been available for years.' He bends down and draws a vacuum pump in the sand.

'Would it be possible for you to bring one with you next time you come?'

'I can try.'

His wife comes out with another basket of clothes,

and he hastily erases the drawing with the sole of his shoe and lowers his eyes.

I get a lift to the centre in a lorry, sitting in the back leaning against the cab and observing the landscape of apartment blocks as they slide past, car parks and play-grounds and news-stands and tea stalls, the sun sinking behind the high blocks and etching them in silhouette, the minarets awakening to life, the cars putting on their lights, the traffic getting heavier and grinding to a halt.

———

On demobilization all my fellow-soldiers and I had the offer of either a school place and a part-time civil service position, or start-up support in cash. Many chose start-up money, I chose a school place and part-time employment.

The job was in the Ministry of Education, first on the switchboard and later as secretary to a departmental head. I familiarized myself with school planning and syllabuses and regulations as they were drafted and after a while my boss began to ask me for advice.

I went to school two days and three evenings a week. I started with technical subjects, practical things, to test myself, and then went on to languages for a while before abandoning both in favour of social sciences and political theory.

In the periods when he lived with me he used to have a meal ready when I came home from my evening classes. I would tell him about what I had learnt, I wanted to try the new concepts out on him. For the most part he just listened, asked an occasional question, continued listening. One evening I spoke enthusiastically about the transition from production for daily consumption to production for stock.

'Imagine an island with five hermits on it. They live by

fishing, hunting and agriculture. Then one day they decide to move in together.'

I took his hand, dipped my finger in his wineglass and drew four lines on his palm: four hermits who moved from their respective corners of the island to join the fifth.

'Why?'

'Because they have realized that together they can achieve more than each working for himself. They have to give up something, but they gain more than they lose.'

'What do they gain?'

'Division of labour increases efficiency.'

'And what do they lose?'

'Freedom. Our lecturer said that this is the cement that binds society together: the members of society have to feel that they get more from being part of society than they have to give. The day they no longer feel that, society disintegrates. Is that right?'

'That's how it seems where I come from.'

I stopped and looked at him, waiting for him to say more. Then I clasped his hand again and continued.

'Eventually the hermits have children with one another and the island society grows. Next comes specialization, the second major step in social development. First, division of labour, then specialization, which together increase efficiency so much that one day society goes over to producing for stock. And that is the great leap in political economy; the island now has a surplus and can exchange with other islands.'

'A sack of potatoes for a crate of beer.'

'Exactly. And at that point not all need participate in production; some can be released and set to work on other things, like education, health or administration.'

'And some on entirely different things.'

I let go his hand.

'Yes. Some on entirely different things.'

'Some can be released and set to work on religion, constructing a system of norms that both justifies the conditions of property ownership in society and ensures the passivity of the people.'

'Yes.'

That night, after we had gone to bed, I whispered to him, 'Do you think that's how it is?'

'Yes and no. I think it's correct to say that religion can be conservative, can be oppressive, can have a deadening effect, but I also think there's one thing that Marxist theory is too cold and hard to incorporate.'

'What's that?'

'Do they dream on the island?'

L ofty skies above an open landscape and the sound of running water. I am not sure whether it was the sound of a river or of tears, my first tears, because when I cry I feel a river inside me, a river that never ceases flowing, leaden and impassive, inexorable.

We were lying in a tent near a waterfall waiting for the local people in an isolated district to assemble for a meeting. The Central Committee had proposed building a dam in the valley, which would change the lives of the locals for ever. We made use of the days to be together, to be on our own. In the mornings he gathered twigs for a small fire and made me tea, and then we sat reading with our feet dangling in the water. In the afternoons we would lie in the shade of a tree and sleep. In the evenings he lit a fire and read aloud to me, usually some piece he had come across and liked. The river flowed past, broad and impassive, and he sat there reading in the light of the fire, the flames reflected in his eyes and voice. Before we went to bed I would ask him to translate the poem to me, the one he kept on a sheet of paper in his left breast pocket. It was like a ritual, like asking him to play a tune for me or make love to me. The poem did something to him, moved him, opened him so that I could see right inside him.

I always sat very close to him when he read it, but not actually touching him; I needed space for the images that came with his voice. When I shut my eyes and think of the poem there is always one image that comes to me: a white horse galloping away in a green meadow. There is something sad about the image, something that is over; when I lean forward I can see that the horse is old. Why is it galloping? Was it frightened? By what?

The poem is about three men travelling to greet a birth. I can see them before me, high up on the backs of camels, day in, day out. It must be a king being born; they ride in the pouring rain and biting cold, through villages that do not like strangers; they end up sleeping in shifts, they dream of summer and silk-clad girls bringing cold drinks, they hit out at the voices whispering that this is madness.

They find the place, I see them riding down from a barren desert into a fertile valley, a little stream and a water-mill beating holes in the darkness. They find the place, and everything would have been all right if the poem had stopped there, but it doesn't: the old white horse gallops away in the green meadow and the three men turn back, he is one of them, I can see that now. They are changed, a quietness has come over them; I ask them if they found the birth, and they nod, and one of them says that he thought birth and death were more different, this birth was like dying. They ride on homewards, gazing around in wonder, as if looking for someone, a familiar face, but find none. Once more I see the old white horse galloping away, and now I know what it represents. And wish I didn't.

I mentioned the poem to two of my teachers: one said it was from Christian mythology and was about the Magi who rode to the stable where the Son of Man was born, the other said the birth symbolized our victory, that the death symbolized all who had given their lives for the victory and that birth and death were thus interrelated. Nonsense. I have sat by a fire next to the person who has read me that poem night after night and I know what he was telling me about: people who went off on a journey and came back changed.

When he had finished he always sat with the piece of paper in his hand looking towards the river without saying anything, and then I knew where he was and I was there with him and that place has a name, but not all names are to be spoken.

Some days goatherds came down to the river with their flocks and let their animals drink while they themselves bathed; on other days women and children came past on their way to or from the market. They stopped to talk to us, intrigued to know what we were doing there. We would sit with them for hours. The women wore skimpy loincloths of animal hide, but were otherwise quite naked, greased with reddish-brown clay as protection against the sun, the children completely naked. We scarcely ever saw any men, and the few we did see were drunk, usually with an automatic rifle slung over their shoulders.

———

Lofty skies above an open landscape and the sound of running water. I am not sure whether it was the sound of a river or an echo within me, the echo of something I knew without words, a leaden, impassive, inexorable certainty.

We had travelled far from everything and used the days to be close to each other; we went for lengthy walks, talked, took it easy. I had seen her in battle, I had seen her storming from one position to the next with a stuttering machine gun in her hands, wild and dangerous; I had seen her in a defence position, seen her taking cover in low concrete bunkers with cement showering down on her from all sides, fearful and panting; now I saw her tender and delicate. In the evenings we lit a fire and sat in silence beneath silent stars. We could sit for hours just being, and if it is true that being is the essence of

133

man, then there is no meaning in life beyond that, being. Before we went to bed she would bless us, every single night. When she got up from the fire and went off into the darkness without a word I knew what was in store and began looking forward to it, the way we look forward to rituals.

She would come back after a while with a snake. The landscape around us was arid semi-desert, and it never took her long to find one. In the light of the fire she would squeeze out the venom into a bowl-shaped leaf: she held the snake in a firm grip behind its head and forced its jaws open, and the white poison fell on to the green leaf in hard angry globules. Then she would kill the snake with one swift slash of her knife and mix some drops of its blood with the venom. I used to study the snake's eyes, looking for a sign of comprehension or fear, but never found it; the snake was killed the way it had killed, with complete indifference.

Having slowly warmed the mixture of blood and venom over the fire, she took a cactus needle, pricked the little finger of her left hand and pressed out a drop of blood. Then she looked at me and nodded, I held out my hand, felt the slight prick and watched our two drops of blood mingle into the red-and-white mixture in the bottom of the leaf. She heated the leaf some more and then dipped her right index finger in the mixture and drew a sign on my forehead, dipped again and drew a sign on her own. Then she took the leaf to the river and sent it off downstream, and came back to me. We sat in silence as the leaf floated away, listened to it calling out, or weeping, once even seeming to glow; and when it had disappeared I always had the feeling of something new, a change, and I always felt something new in the woman by my side. The smell of her and the taste of her had been part of what had most attracted me, and when we lay down to sleep I could detect a new smell and a new taste, every night, the smell of spices and incense, the taste of oils and salts.

One night I heard myself whisper, just as I was going off to sleep, 'That's how people kill, too, with complete indifference,' and she turned and looked at me and put her hand on my arm.

Lofty skies above an open landscape and the sound of a great throng. People had been arriving in droves since before dawn, mostly on foot, but some in clapped-out buses. Some were naked, some wore socks and shoes, some a European hat, some children's yellow plastic sunglasses, some were fully dressed in dark suits with waistcoats.

They settled under an enormous fig tree a little way from the river; its roots extended fifteen to twenty metres outwards from the trunk above the ground, forming natural benches. They sat or lay in the shade of the tree, some sleeping, some eating, some talking. The sun rose in the sky, the early morning breeze died down and the heat of the day descended like a blanket over the landscape.

She had put on her uniform. I sat and looked at her: she was a different person from my companion of the last few days. She was with a group of others in uniform, men and women, standing at a slight remove from the people under the fig tree. She was straighter in the back, more decisive in her movements, sharper-eyed. A Land Rover appeared with five whites aboard, European nature conservationists, and she measured them up coolly. She glanced across at me occasionally, as if to make sure I was still there, and once or twice she came over to speak to me. I was proud of her, she was so elegant; elegant and somehow daunting.

People were still crowding in. By the time the sun was overhead there must have been two hundred beneath the tree. The Central Committee had put out tables and chairs and there were five officers with a flip-chart and pointer. They stood up in turn, drew on the big white sheets of paper and indicated with the pointer as they addressed the people under the tree. One of them unrolled a map, another had ready-made tabulations in four colours. The people under the tree followed everything attentively but in silence.

When the last officer had finished, an elderly man rose from the tree-root he had been sitting on, just a few metres from the panel of officers. He reached up and hung on to a branch as if to support himself, a gesture that gave him an air of relaxed authority that brought a dark glint to the officers' eyes.

I had found someone who could interpret, he was right behind me whispering in my ear.

'That's the chief. He's been chief ever since he reached manhood.'

'What's he saying?'

'He hasn't started speaking yet.'

The chief was wearing a shabby brown suit, black shoes and a chunky necklace of red-and-white plastic pearls. His hair was crinkly grey, his face thin and taut, his eyes two burning brown slits. He began to speak calmly and without raising his voice, like a man who was used to being listened to. The interpreter gave me a simultaneous translation.

'As chief of all the clans up here, it is an honour for me to welcome you as emissaries from the capital. We realize you have had a lengthy journey to come here, and we want you to know that we much appreciate the attention you are according us.'

The officers smiled in affirmation.

The chief continued, 'There are long intervals between the occasions we see you here, but when you come, it always lights a lamp in our existence, because we know we have something you want, and that is the greatest gift in life, to have something to give to others.

'The first time we saw you was during the civil war. You wanted our young boys then, and you got them. Many of them never came back, but the country was freed. They gave their lives so that we can be as we are now, free people.'

The officers nodded solemnly.

'The second time we saw you was during the preparations for this visit, when you sent scouts to draw maps and ask questions. They drew maps everywhere, day after day, and they put questions to everyone, men and women, children and the elderly; they wrote the answers in thick books, and helped themselves avidly to our women. That brought many bad things for us, but more that was good, because a man can be proud when he has something to give to emissaries from the capital – land, an answer, a woman.

'Now you are here again, and this time you want our valley. This time you want to build a dam across the gorge where the waterfall flows and put our valley under water so that the capital can have electricity.'

He paused. The officers watched him tensely.

'This time you have brought a gift yourselves, a generous gift, which may mean that what you want from us is important to you, more important than our young men and our young women.'

The officers cast their eyes down.

'Why else would you come to me after dark last night and give me this?'

The chief had a leather portfolio handed up to him, unfastened the zip and turned it upside down. Bundles of banknotes tied with strips of white paper came tumbling out and a gasp went up from the audience like a shock wave. The officers stared at the chief, their faces rigid.

'My dear friends from the capital, what can I do with this? Can I buy back my son from the grave with this? Can I buy back my daughter's virginity? If I let you put our valley under water, can I use this to buy myself peace from my ancestors who are buried here?'

The officers sat stony-faced. The chief pushed the bank-notes towards them with his foot.

'Up here, we pay with animals when we trade, a goat for a sack of sweet potatoes, two cows for a sack of corn. But you obviously prefer using people as payment, our young boys as payment for peace, our young women as payment for devel-opment. So give me that, give me people: a thousand young men and women, and the valley is yours.'

My interpreter added a comment of his own. 'That was what Genghis Khan demanded and got from the Jin Emperor in the siege of Zhongdu.'

I nodded.

The chief had sat down. The officers sat as if stunned for a full minute before starting to confer. The people under the fig tree were talking animatedly, many of them clapping their hands and laughing. One of the officers stood up and came forward, and the chief raised his hand for silence. The officer called over an interpreter, a thin frail lad in camouflage uniform.

'Chief, it is a great honour for us to be here today, and we are full of gratitude for your constructive contribution to our dialogue. We promise to pass it on to our superiors in the capital, but we venture to say even now that your proposal will in all likelihood be rejected. The Central Committee does not engage in human barter. We do not ourselves feel entirely convinced that your suggestion is intended for serious consideration, and if this is so, if it is intended as mockery, what would your ancestors say of such treatment of your guests?'

The chief rose and began to dance with closed eyes, humming in a slow monotone as he clapped his hands and swayed back and forth, took a few steps to one side, stretched up his arms in an appeal to heaven. Alarm spread among the listeners, those sitting furthest away were the first to notice something, and it was coming nearer, people touched the ground and looked at one another in acknowledgement: the ground was moving, a muffled powerful rumble increasing in intensity, now the officers felt it too, and they stared at the flower in the empty lemonade bottle on one of the tables: the bottle was quivering, began to bounce, toppled over.

The taste of anger and hot blood rising, the sound of cold, harsh voices, a terrible sound, because it was not new voices, not strangers' voices, but our own that had changed. We had travelled out to a country village for an election meeting, he as a reporter, I as a representative of the Party. It was a Muslim village, poor and populous. In my country the Muslims live on the lowland and the Christians on the high plateau. A village of dice-playing men and enclosed courtyards, my own people, but from long, long ago.

He asked to be set down as we approached the village; he didn't want to come driving in. I have wondered since whether it was us he didn't want to come driving in with. The Council of Elders were sitting under the assembly tree on the edge of the marketplace, and had probably been sitting there since early morning. We greeted them and handed them gifts; they greeted us and handed us gifts. They asked us to sit down, six of us from the Party and four armed soldiers; there were eighteen of them. We had checked that in advance; it was important for us not to outnumber them.

Four young boys brought out tea and dried fruit. I could feel I was being watched from the tops of walls round the enclosed courtyards, from heavy wooden doors cautiously ajar.

My five colleagues from the Party were all men, two of the soldiers were women; three women and seven men –

that too was important: the Council of Elders consisted only of men.

The senior one among them stood up and stepped forward a few paces. He was a handsome grey-bearded man in a white robe, carrying the staff of seniority made of polished ebony with a silver cap. I knew that many senior councillors used to hollow out the staff and insert the relics of their forefathers to give them power. You could see who had and who hadn't by observing their knuckles as they held the staff: white knuckles indicated relics.

He began by relating the history of the village and the clan for three generations back, who had gone away, who had returned, who had been born and who had died. He pointed out their lands to us and told us who was cultivating them this year. The land was allocated each year by the Council of Elders. He told us of their plans for the village: a small mosque, a village hall where the boys could learn the Koran, a new well.

The village Elder sat down and the oldest of our colleagues from the Party stood up. He responded by recounting the history of the country and the people for three generations back. He told of freedom under the king, of the sudden attack by foreign soldiers, of the king's flight, of all the years of repression, of the liberation movement and life at the front, of victory and plans for the future.

'Now the new time has arrived. Now we can rebuild the country. We are here today to involve you in electing a government to make laws and choose a president.'

He sat down. He was a good speaker, with a deep voice, broad shoulders and large hands. The Council of Elders murmured amongst themselves while we sat in silence. After a while their senior man rose again.

'Permit me to ask: why do we want a president when we have a king, why do we need a government when we have the king's men, why laws that we already have?'

Our spokesman stood up. He was a mild-mannered man, selected with care.

'The king is still in exile, in another country, and we don't know whether he'll ever return. In the meantime the country has to be governed.'

'Can't the clan leaders govern for the time being?'

The senior village Elder had positioned himself right in front of our spokesman.

'The Christians in the highlands are not divided into clans.'

'Well, let them decide how they want to be governed.'

'We need one united government for the whole country.'

'Why?'

'Because only then will we be strong enough to solve the really major problems: schools, hospitals, roads.'

The senior Elder went back to his Council and they conferred in low voices for a while before he returned to speak again.

'The Council of Elders have asked me to choose a representative for the government. I give you Ahmed al Noor, an honest and clever man, as was his father before him and his grandfather before him.'

'That's not quite the way it's done. We have brought a list of men you can choose from.'

Our spokesman held up a piece of paper. The senior Elder put on his spectacles and studied it.

'These are all strangers. How can we elect strangers to a council that has to solve what you call the really major problems?'

'We are the ones who compiled the list, we can vouch for them.'

'If it is you who have compiled the list and you who vouch for them, why can't you also vote for them?'

The taste of anger and hot blood rising, the sound of cold, harsh voices, a terrible sound, because it was not new voices, not strangers' voices, but our own that had changed. I sat there and saw her lie and knew that we had something to confront, I sat and saw her lie for the first time and felt something break inside me. I tried to catch her eye, but she was not looking in my direction, just sitting there among her delegation, two armed soldiers on each side.

'Why didn't you say anything?'

We had waited until we were back in the capital and alone; we hadn't talked much on the return journey, a loaded, unpleasant silence.

'Why didn't you say anything?'

'What did you want me to say?'

'The king isn't coming back because the liberation movement doesn't want him back, you know that.'

'What did you want me to say? Should I have stood up, a woman, spoken unbidden to the Council of Elders, criticizing their king and telling them he was a crook? We don't do that here.'

'And why didn't your people answer honestly when he asked why you didn't elect the government yourselves? If it was you who compiled the list of candidates and you who vouched for them — you might as well bloody elect them.'

'I won't have you swearing at me.'

'Well, I'm doing it now.'

'You're as aware as I am what would happen if we left them a free choice. They would elect friends and family, people they're in debt to or people they can expect a reciprocal favour from. Do you think we've fought all these years to reintroduce the same old corrupt system?'

'That wasn't what I was asking.'

'We want to build a democracy in this country, that's why we want their participation in the election.'

'It's not democracy to dictate to people who they should vote for. But you have to look like a democracy in order to get international recognition and access to millions in aid money.'

'One thing I won't have is you shouting at me. I've grown up with men who've shouted at me and I don't want any more of it, do you hear, so don't shout at me.'

'Belief in fate.'

She was lying with her head on my stomach. I saw the words come out of her mouth tinged deep purple and rise towards the ceiling with the blue nutmeg smoke, where they were split in two by the fan and sent in different directions, fate in one, belief in the other. She repeated the words and the same thing happened.

'Here.'

She held out the rolled cigarette towards me, slowly, her eyes blurred. I shook my head and the motion made the colours in my brain blend together. I had put them in such good order, and now all was confusion again.

'*Insha'Allah.* If God wills.'

In-sha-Allah. She didn't say it right. *In-sha-Allah.* There was more yellow in it. More yellow and a hint of green.

'*Insha'Allah. Insha'Allah, insha'Allah, insha'Allah.* I have grown up with *insha'Allah*, I live with *insha'Allah*, I shall die with *insha'Allah.* Not historical inevitability, but *insha'Allah.*'

I put a green frame round the words 'historical inevitability'. I had seen them before, where I grew up myself, green for hope, green for integrity.

'People fall sick if God wills, they succumb to accidents if God wills, they die if God wills. People get work if God wills, lose their jobs if God wills, go to war if God wills, win if God wills, lose if God wills. What else?'

143

'Smoke nutmeg if God wills.'

'Smoke nutmeg if God wills.'

She took a long drag on the cigarette and let the smoke percolate from her mouth up into her nose.

'Is it afternoon?'

'I think so.'

She lifted her head and looked at me, twisted on to one elbow and manoeuvred herself over me with her eyes fixed on mine, a little wild now. She took both my hands and pushed them under my back, lay full length on top of me with her face close to mine and whispered in my ear, 'This is what it's like living with *insha'Allah.*'

I could feel that she had my legs in a lock; I tried to move, but she just smiled and held me down.

'If I let you move, it's because I want to, not you; if I let you go, it's because I want to, not you; if I unbutton your shirt, it's because I want to, not you.'

She carefully undid two buttons and inserted her hand.

'When you've lain like this for a hundred years you'll have some idea of what it's like to be a woman, but only some; when you've lain like this for another hundred years you'll have some idea of what it's like to be a believer, but only some; and when you've lain like this for yet another hundred years, you too won't take it any more, because it's against human nature to lie like that; then you'll start experimenting with evil spirits and protective hands and herbs and unguents and the Evil Eye, then you'll get a marabout with *baraka*, spiritual power, to write down quotations from the Holy Book in chalk on a board and give you the water he washes them off with so that you can drink it, or sprinkle it on the floor. When you've lain like this for three hundred years, you'll do anything to get yourself up, to set yourself free, because you won't be able to bear it any longer. Every time a religious or political leader goes by, and for us they're one and

144

the same, you'll cry *insha'Allah*, because that's what you know he wants to hear, but as soon as he has gone past you'll try to get aid from spirits to help you to your feet.'

She caught the word 'spirits' as she said it and held it right in front of my eyes with a smile. It sparkled as she waved it to and fro and she undid two more buttons on my shirt and rammed it in; I felt it sting. She gripped both my wrists under my back with one hand and put the other on my brow, pressed my head against the floor and sank her teeth sharply into my throat, heard me scream, laughed and bit again.

'I can crush your windpipe so that you can't breathe, or sever your artery and let your heart pump you dry, I can jab my knee into your groin, like this, while I shake you and shout at you that you're not to engage in necromancy, do you hear, you're not to engage in necromancy, because that is interfering with God's plan, criticizing God. But at the same time I do nothing to stop you, because I know that as long as you engage in necromancy you will remain prostrate, it won't occur to you that you can help yourself up; and people who call out to you that you can, that you must, they are heathens, so you won't listen to them; meanwhile I console you and you are content to lie where you are.'

She undid the last buttons on my shirt. Her voice caressed my skin.

'It's a question of power, my friend, power. For caliphs and imams power is an end in itself, not a means to anything else, because power is the very proof that they have won, that they have succeeded in subjecting a society to their will. They have power because they have made people accept their description of reality, both internal and external; they have power because they have managed to appropriate for themselves a monopoly on defining which world is the real one.'

I tried to wriggle free. I don't like people lying on top of me

and talking about which world is the real one; it has something to do with the colour of the words.

'We won the war, but we didn't win them; we have
external power, but not internal; we can introduce political
and economic reforms as much as we like, but if the mullah or
the imam in the local mosque doesn't give his approval we
won't get far. And even with their support there's no
guarantee that we'll succeed, because beyond the mosques,
in village-reality, people listen just as much to voices other
than those of the mullah or the imam. They listen to the
Council of Elders, to the spirits of their forefathers, to jinn that
speak in the night; and they don't want any changes, not
because they're against anything new in principle, but because
traditions have been handed down by their forefathers, and
the spirits of the dead can be angered or even incited to take
revenge if what they have bequeathed is changed.'

She let go of my hands and put them round herself,
touched my lips with her fingers.

'Power corrupts. Who was it who said that?'

'Wasn't it one of your people?'

She took a drag on her cigarette, put her lips to mine and
blew in. A taste of nutmeg, of her, of power.

'Will you dream a dream for me?'

She rolled over as she spoke, slowly and intimately.

'About power?'

She nodded and put her arm beneath my head; I turned
towards her and looked at her, then lifted her up and
carried her with me, followed the taste of nutmeg and the
taste of her, and carried her towards the taste of power,
towards the strongest power the world has ever known, the
Mongols.

In Samarkand there is a centre for European sperm. Not
many people know that; I don't believe even the

authorities know. I know because a woman took me there when she found out I was a European.

'Russian?'

She has a shrill, piercing voice.

'No.'

'American?'

'No.'

'But you're a great conversationalist, that's for sure.'

She slaps me on the back so hard that I drop my notebook and pencil. I am sitting in a corner of the courtyard of Bibi Khanum, the Queen's Mosque, making notes. In the centre of the courtyard is a massive Koran lectern shaped like an open book. A constant stream of women has been coming all afternoon and crawling under the lectern, first three times one way and then three times the other. Now and again a man comes and walks round it twice, clockwise, muttering something. I indicate them with a nod of my head.

'The people crawling under it?'

'Back pain or wishing for many children.'

'And walking round it?'

'Some other wish.'

She gives me another mighty thump, and then bends down and whispers, 'I've heard you have a sport called dwarf-throwing. When you run out of dwarfs you can have Mongols from us. How many would you like? Ten million? Twenty million?'

'I'm not Australian.'

'What are you then?'

'European.'

She steps back to take a better look at me.

'I thought Europeans were younger.'

She is a big woman in a black skirt and red windcheater, beneath which she wears a check shirt with a gold cross hanging at the open neck. Her hair is dark and curly, with a trace of grey; her eyes blue, very blue, her face thin. She puts her head slightly on one side, as if half-jocularly, and asks:

'What's your sperm like?'

'Neither better nor worse than anyone else's, I suppose. What about yours?'

'Watch it.'

'Sorry.'

She takes my arm and leads me off, across the Registan, the most famous square in Central Asia, and down ulitsa Registankaya, a monument to Russian concrete architecture. A forest of TV aerials rises above the walls of the grey apartment blocks and petrol and diesel fumes hang over the potholed streets.

She steers me into a narrow side street and stops at a door, rings a bell and waits. The house could be from the Turkish period, with rich ornamentation and a door that was once blue. A face peers through a hatch, nods, and the door opens. It is a slim young woman in apron and slippers. We follow her up a flight of stairs and through another door.

'The Centre for European Perpetuation?'

I glance enquiringly at the sign on the door as we go in.

'Yes. This is it.'

The room is small and cramped with peeling green paint on the wainscoting, a cupboard full of test-tubes, an old rusting freezer, a desk and a stool. On the desk shoeboxes of index cards are piled on top of one another to a height of about a metre, and on the stool is a silver samovar. The woman in apron and slippers opens the cupboard, takes out three test-tubes, goes

148

over to the samovar and fills them with tea, hands one to me, one to the woman in the red windcheater, and raises her own.

'God bless King and Fatherland.'

She brings the heels of her slippers together in salute. The woman in the red windcheater picks up a tambourine from the desk drawer, taps it experimentally against the palm of her hand and starts singing and marching up and down to a steady rhythm. The woman in apron and slippers joins in with a counterpoint and both march back and forth with an expectant look.

'*Alte Kameraden?*'

'That's right.'

They exchange joyful glances: a genuine European at last. One of them sings the althorn, the other the tuba blasts; the tambourine is shaken on the third beat of each bar, giving the march a strange stumbling character. The woman in the red windcheater hitches up her skirt.

'We dance this dance for all our donors, it's part of the perpetuation process. For donors who've travelled here we dance it naked. Would you like that?'

'It's not necessary.'

The freezer motor suddenly judders into action and the two women shriek. The one with the red windcheater throws down the tambourine, runs over to the cupboard and puts her arms round it, the one in apron and slippers shouts at the freezer and kicks it. The test-tubes start to vibrate, first slowly and hesitantly and then faster and more resolutely.

'This damned freezer has cost us eight hundred test-tubes. Lousy Mongolian freezer. Would you like to see our donor album?'

The woman in the red windcheater nods towards the desk. I open the drawer and pull out a black leather album with engraved gold letters: *Europa Fidelis*. There is a map of Europe on the first page, apparently late Middle Ages, then a hundred pages of men's faces, twenty to a page, with name and date of birth, first sketched and tinted, before the time of photography, then in faded sepia, then clearer black-and-white and finally in colour, gaudy and out of focus.

The pictures are like a journey through time, clothes and background tell of epochs, hairstyles and moustaches of self-image. Some smile, some are serious, some stern. I take out my notebook and write a few words, the woman in the red windcheater watching inquisitively.

'What are you writing?'

'Just something that struck me. Everyone in the pictures has such wide-open eyes.'

'That's part of the training. We don't want to turn into this.'

She lets go of the cupboard, puts a finger in the corner of each eye and pulls outwards.

The test tubes are still clinking alarmingly.

'Is there anything else that strikes you?'

'Yes, one thing. The hair.'

The freezer motor suddenly cuts out, as if I have said something unforgivable, and the two women stand looking at me. Then they both come over to me with a slightly mournful, dejected air and sit on the edge of the desk. They glance at one another as if to see who should begin. It is the woman in the red windcheater.

'Genghis Khan's grandson Batu Khan advanced the furthest into Europe. Bulgaria, Russia, Poland, Moravia, Silesia, Hungary; he swept all before him. And he had one particular habit: he collected young girls from every country he conquered, young, untouched girls from

150

good families, and took them to his headquarters. They were housed there according to geographical provenance: here the Arab harem, there the Indian, there the Persian, the Russian, the European.

'At first they were kept under lock and key. Batu Khan sent for them every morning and every evening when he was in his headquarters; he never learnt their names, but just told his bodyguard to fetch ten of each, and would amuse himself with them for a few hours before selecting three or four. The others were sent back.

'Eventually the girls were allowed out into the city, always attended by two eunuchs, but relatively free. They were shocked by what they saw: a city where open sewers flowed through the streets and slaves were sold publicly. On their walks in the city they also heard news of the Great Khan's latest victories, and they realized that in all probability they would remain concubines for the rest of their lives. It was then they drew up the Great European Sperm Project.'

'The Great European Sperm Project?'

'Yes. The European girls couldn't stand Mongols, but had no choice, so they asked themselves how they could best preserve their European identity, as an act of defiance towards the Mongols. They began with cultural evenings; they got hold of spinets and other stringed instruments and books, they played folk music, read to one another, spoke about the cultures of their countries of origin. Instruments and books were easy to come by, because the markets in the city were bulging with plundered goods from the campaigns, and the girls had a method of payment that was much in demand: the Great Khan's soldiers competed for the job of guarding the harem and running errands for them.

'The cultural evenings had their effect. The girls

became more and more European, more and more refined. That titillated the Khan, who like most men was attracted to the exotic. But the girls realized that European culture would die out with them unless they could get European sperm.'

'And the Mongols hadn't been able to plunder that on their campaigns?'

'Well, they had in a way. The Mongols were an uneducated race of horsemen, but they knew what knowledge was and they took it back with them: Chinese engineers, Arabian architects, Indian traders, European craftsmen. Samarkand had more than enough European sperm, the only problem was how to get it into the harem.'

'Every age has its own peculiar problems.'

'The solution in this case was unconventional.'

'That's enough.'

She took my arm and shook it, sat up and reached out for the tobacco pouch and the nutmeg bowl. I rested my hand on her back, stroked her lightly with my fingers.

'We all know the conventional way sperm comes into a harem. We don't want to hear about the unconventional.'

She lay down again while she rolled a cigarette.

'Something's happening to your stories, did you know that? It frightens me a bit.'

She moved nearer to me and held the cigarette in the air. I looked at her. She closed her eyes; in her culture it is not polite to stare, but I wasn't staring, I was looking at her, and that is different, that is communicating. She opened her eyes and looked at me a little uncertainly. In the distance I could hear a thundering noise, as of horses or tanks. She put the cigarette to my lips and I drew on it without averting my gaze; her eyes had always fascinated me.

'What's that sound?'

'The Mongols are coming. "And the fifth angel sounded, and I saw a star fall from heaven unto the earth: and to him was given the key of the bottomless pit. And he opened the bottomless pit; and there arose a smoke out of the pit, as the smoke of a great furnace; and the sun and the air were darkened by reason of the smoke of the pit. And there came out of the smoke locusts upon the earth: and unto them was given power, as the scorpions of the earth have power. And it was commanded them that they should not hurt the grass of the earth, neither any green thing, neither any tree; but only those men which have not the seal of God in their foreheads. And to them it was given that they should not kill them, but that they should be tormented five months: and their torment was as the torment of a scorpion, when he striketh a man. And in those days shall men seek death, and shall not find it; and shall desire to die, and death shall flee from them. And the shapes of the locusts were like unto horses prepared unto battle; and on their heads were as it were crowns like gold, and their faces were as the faces of men. And they had hair as the hair of women, and their teeth were as the teeth of lions. And they had breastplates, as it were breastplates of iron; and the sound of their wings was as the sound of chariots of many horses running to battle. And they had tails like unto scorpions, and there were stings in their tails: and their power was to hurt men five months." Revelation of St John, 9, 1–10.'

She sat up and stubbed out her cigarette.

'That's enough revelation for today.'

She lay down again with her back pressed up against me and my arms around her. I closed my eyes and hugged her, closed my eyes and listened to the thundering, much nearer now, I could see them; they weren't horses, they weren't tanks, they were scorpions with slanting eyes.

'What is it?'

She had turned and put her hand on my arm.

'Was I twitching?'

'Yes.'

'I must have been dreaming.'

She rolled over completely and put her hands on my head.

'You dream the whole time now.'

We lay like that for a while, quite still, until the echo of the thundering noise had died down and the colours disappeared, until my breathing was calmer and the tears were running slower, hers or mine.

A cool afternoon and the fresh smell that follows rain. We were sitting on the verandah with an espresso each and the silent bond between us that sleep during the day brings. A camel caravan passed the house, a car tooted, from the minaret came the call to prayer. The sun was on its way down, shining obliquely between the houses and bathing everything in a golden light.

'What is the essence of power?'

I listened to my own question for a moment before attempting an answer, which is no bad rule.

'Spinoza wrote that the essence of a thing is the quality of the thing that the thing cannot lack without ceasing to be that thing.'

'Well said.'

'What is it about power that makes it power? Aristotle maintained that politics starts with the meeting of two people, because that's when the competition for power begins. Bertrand Russell wrote on the paradox of competition that "the aim of all competition is to eliminate the competition". That must mean that the challenge for everyone who competes is to become so strong that the competitors are annihilated and the competition eradicated. But what does it mean, that the competitors are annihilated? Physically or psychologically? Both, presumably. And the one not only presupposes but also reinforces the other. In the thirteenth century, when the Mongols invaded Europe, every description of their brutality was believed implicitly. The monk Ivo of Narbonne wrote from Austria that "virgins were raped until they died of exhaustion, after which their breasts were cut off and served as delicacies to Mongol chiefs". Europeans had no doubt of what awaited them; contemporary historians had already reported systematic slaughter in towns that the Mongols had conquered: seven hundred thousand in Merv, one million, six hundred thousand in Herat, one million, seven hundred and forty-seven thousand in Nishapur. In some places it was said that the Mongols slaughtered everything, even cats and dogs, so that the towns simply ceased to exist. In others it was reported that they drove the populace before them as human shields to the next battle zone.

'It may have been this psychological supremacy that led to the establishment of the Mongols in the course of three hundred years as the biggest empire the world has ever seen: China, India, Persia, Caucasus, Russia and large parts of Europe. The reputation of the Mongols preceded them and cleared the way, and the Christian Church played into their hands; priests told their terrified congregations that the Mongols were God's punishment for the sins of the world, in other words they got what they deserved. And who dares resist a just punishment?'

Dreaming water. No one goes there, no one fishes there, dreaming water, Djimdjim. The Moon and Djabo had created it with song on their way south. They had followed the ridges and given places names, they had cut bamboo canes as fishing rods, made *galaidjidji* bags to put their belongings in and woven bands of hair to wear round their bodies and foreheads.

Djimdjim. He was telling me about the first journey. We were sitting under a straw roof with a glass of tea between us, waiting for a bus. It might come today or tomorrow or next week. Djimdjim. Eyes watched us from every doorway in the village.

The story began with the Moon and Djabo travelling south, down from the sea-water coast. They were looking for a place, a country, and they pitched camp many times and gave places names, they planted almond lotus, they created places and fish and red lilies, they pulled out their beard hairs and planted them and they grew into spear-grasses; they created a great open lake, almost like the sea. No one goes there, no one fishes there, it is taboo, dreaming water. They made it taboo and dangerous, and it is still taboo and dangerous. They created land with song, they sang to the hills and changed their shape, sang to the rivers and altered their course, sang to the plains and raised them up, and so they created a broad open lake, dreaming water, no one goes there, no one fishes there, they made it taboo and dangerous.

'Why?'

'I don't know.'

He didn't know.

The Moon and Djabo went on travelling, went on creating, they discarded their old languages, the languages of their mothers and fathers, and spoke new languages. Listening to themselves one day, they began to feel unwell. They ceased their wanderings and rested, did not go hunting. They said, 'We will lie down here to die, our bodies will remain here, in Djawun and Mayali lands. We have forsaken our mothers and fathers, our grandparents, they are far away, we have almost forgotten them. We have lost our links to them, and when we die, who will take them the news of our death?'

He looked up and saw the question, without surprise, who will take them the news of our death? The eyes watching us from every doorway saw it too, who will take them the news of our death? Djabo died first; the Moon went on breathing for a while. He was a strong man, a clever man, a *margidbu*. He said, 'I shall die, and then I shall come back, in another body, yet still my own.' Djabo simply lay there, his body dead for all time. The Moon could have brought him back to life, but Djabo did not trust the Moon and thought it was a trick.

'And then the Moon died too. They could have followed him and done as he did, those first men. They saw him rise as a new moon. When he was high in the sky, men and women and children called out, pleased to see him. "Yes indeed," they shouted, "this Moon, he is a hero, a *margidbu*. He rises, he holds up the sky, we see him, he dies, and then he comes back again. That Djabo, he simply died for all time, he just lay there as a dead body, but the Moon brought himself back to life. We see him every day, his body dies for three days and then we see him again as a new moon. We could have done as he did, could have been like him, but Djabo spoilt things for us when he died for all time, and now they bury our bodies, just as the Moon said." '

A long pause before he went on:

'They formed the landscape with song, they depicted death as mankind's choice, and they were the first to make a connection between recognition and reality; a thing is not real until it is recognized; and who would take back the news of their death, and in what language, they had left their old language behind.'

Another long pause before he lay down and said, 'A thing is not real until it is told,' and there was a resonance in the words, a very special resonance, and I wondered which he was, the Moon or Djabo, and whether I would ever know, *insha'Allah*, but above all I was certain now where he was going: dreaming water; not to find out why the Moon and Djabo had made the water taboo, but to find out what the dreams were.

'And the water?'

'Is the beginning of the first chapter in the Holy Book.'

'The Koran?'

'The Bible. "Darkness was upon the face of the deep. And the Spirit of God moved upon the face of the waters. And God said, Let there be a firmament in the midst of the waters, and let it divide the waters from the waters. And God made the firmament, and divided the waters which were under the firmament from the waters which were above the firmament: and it was so." Genesis, 1, 2–7.'

'That was the first day?'

'The second.'

'Genesis, chapter one, second day. What did he create on the first day?'

'Light.'

'But water was there before light?'

'Yes. According to ancient Israelite tradition there was originally a primeval ocean that covered everything. That primeval ocean, in the first Greek translation called the abyss, was an image of the underworld, which also incorporated the realm of the dead, where evil spirits could be banished until the end of time.'

'Water above and beneath the heaven?'

'Yes. "In the six hundredth year of Noah's life, in the second month, the seventeenth day of the month, the same day were all the fountains of the great deep broken up, and the windows of heaven were opened." Genesis, 1, 11.'

'But if the water was already there, what about creation?'

'God put limits on the water. In Genesis God says, "Let the waters under the heaven be gathered together unto one place, and let the dry land appear." And it was so, chapter one, verse nine. In the Book of Psalms it says:

> Thou coveredst it with the deep as with a garment:
> The waters stood above the mountains.
> At thy rebuke they fled;
> At the voice of thy thunder they hasted away.
> They go up by the mountains; they go down by the
> valleys
> Unto the place which thou hast founded for them.
> Thou hast set a bound that they may not pass over;
> That they turn not again to cover the earth.

Psalm 104, 6–10.'

'These numbers, do they have to be spoken?'

'Yes.'

'What happens if you leave them out?'

'Then I lose something.'

'And that is no good?'

'No.'

'And when all these numbers have been said and all these thoughts thought, what are you left with?'

'Water that dreams. Water came before everything, before light, before time, before Creation. And water dreamed, because the Spirit of God moved upon it, the way an angel spreads its wings over a sleeping child.'

In Lisbon part of the harbour slopes down towards the sea. The cobbles have been worn smooth and dark after many centuries of bare feet, and now it looks like an enormous abandoned slipway. Behind it is a large square, also covered in smooth cobbles, and an arcaded palace two hundred metres in length. The palace likewise has an abandoned air.

We had travelled to Lisbon together; there was something he wanted to show me. We stood looking across the slipway and out over the endless ocean, he with his arm round me from behind and a hand over my eyes.

'Can you hear anything?'

'Something creaking?'

'It's the hawsers. Can you smell anything?'

I sniffed.

'Sweat?'

'It's the slaves.'

'Spices? Silk?'

'Plundered from the Asian colonies. Can you see the ship?'

He took his hand from my eyes. I opened them.

'What sort of ship is it?'

'Originally a barque, halfway between a schooner and a full-rigger. But the Portuguese started using the caravel in the fifteenth century, with its high structure fore and aft. The Indonesians, Africans and Indians thought the caravels were emissaries of the gods when they first appeared on the horizon. They soon learnt otherwise.'

I contemplated the red-painted ship with the furled brown

sails and the white figurehead, contemplated the black slaves with bare torsos rolling wooden barrels and carrying tea chests and bales of cotton up the slipway, contemplated the sailors hanging over the rail; then I turned round and put my hands on his shoulders, raised myself on tiptoe and studied the horse-drawn carriage with its driver and passenger, a man with long white hair and embroidered finery.

'He looks so pale.'

'He's powdered.'

I looked at the ship again.

'Why must Europeans plunder everything they come across, even at the risk of their lives?'

'It's in our nature.'

We sat on the quayside and I took off my shoes and paddled my toes in the water. The harbour was empty, the square deserted, autumnal. A ship appeared on the horizon, the outline of a modern tanker.

'So the ships sailed empty and returned a few months later with bulging holds?'

'Yes.'

'And you became richer and richer?'

'Yes.'

'While others got poorer and poorer?'

'Yes.'

'For hundreds of years.'

'Yes.'

'Without it occurring to anyone that it was wrong.'

He went down to the sea, gathered some water in his hands, came back to me and bathed my face. I smiled and turned my face to the sun.

'For us Europeans water and sea have always been bound up with dreams. We think there is a continent, a vanished Atlantis at the bottom of the ocean. We found our riches on the other side of the ocean.'

He pointed towards the horizon.

'Cuzco is out there, over the other side, the ancient capital of the Incas. That is where the old and the new world met. I've read the Incas' own account of the behaviour of the first Europeans when they saw the golden treasures in the temples. They became quite manifestly psychotic. They called the Inca king *El dorado*, "the gilded one". It was said that he had himself smeared every day with costly resin as a base for the gold dust that was blown over him with a pipe until it covered his whole body from top to toe.'

'Is Cuzco next?'

He nodded. We stood up and walked into the city, had something to eat in a café, strolled on. If any of our friends had seen us, they would perhaps have said we had slowed down, were less animated. Our movements were still the same, I think, there was still a visible closeness between us, but now we shared long silences.

We stopped outside a theatre and tried to read the poster. I ran my finger over it for words that looked like ballet. I had become totally spellbound by the classical in particular, the disciplined forms that were so different from anything I had seen before. He liked sitting by my side and following the ballet with me, he said he was almost able to feel something moving in me, released by the dancing on stage, something at times dangerous, at times reassuring.

At concerts it was different. I would sit for ages watching him, and he seemed to be aware of it even though he had his eyes shut. There was a mixture of tenderness and fear in my heart. I once told a friend that he seemed to be surrendering himself to the music, there and only there daring to let go; I knew it did him good, but equally I was afraid of what was happening to him. My friend just shook her head.

We spoke no more of the warning lamp I had lit; it wasn't necessary, it was burning brightly enough. Sometimes we were so far away from it that we couldn't see it, sometimes it was as if it didn't exist. Sometimes I regretted having lit it, sometimes he seemed to have forgotten it. But mostly it shone bright and clear, and I knew he had told his friends he felt he had less and less time.

—————

New Cuzco Hotel, base camp for backpackers wanting to see the ruins of the Inca capital. They are collected at dawn by ex-military open trucks, spend two days away and return in the evening of the second day, silent and expressionless. I go along one morning, sit in the back of the truck with six others and enjoy the breeze in my face and the cool night air still clinging to the darkness, and one of them comes over and sits next to me. It is unusual, as backpackers prefer to talk to one another.

'Hi, mister.'

She has a German accent and is whispering.

'Which are the four dimensions?'

A first ray of sun suddenly breaks through the trees and shines in her eyes, they are attractive and slightly drowsy. I lean towards her and whisper in reply, 'Point, line, surface and space, if you count four; width, height and depth if you only count three. Why do you ask?'

'Because we're on our way to the fifth dimension, and I think it's stupid to go there without knowing which are the four we're coming from.'

There is an aroma of soap and toothpaste about her. She has fastened her hair, thick blond hair, with a clasp at the nape of her neck.

'Who's on the way there?'

'We are.'

She makes a circular gesture with her hand which embraces the whole group on the back of the truck.

'I thought we were on our way to the Inca ruins.'

'Yes, of course. And that's where the fifth dimension is. Wait and see. Do you like my breasts?'

'They're fine.'

'You don't think they're too small?'

'They're just right.'

'My friend Dorothea over there, she's had silicon implants put in hers. Do you like hers better?'

'Hard to say in the dark.'

We sit side by side without speaking for a while as the sun climbs above the trees and the ridge of hills, and the truck toils up the steep gravel road. Scattered along the route are little shanties with corrugated-iron roofs, outside which women crouch on their haunches wafting life into fires with big green leaves. I study the backpackers on the truck. Dorothea is standing up front leaning against the cab and looking straight ahead; two Australian boys and an American girl sit facing the other way. At the rear lies a Dutch boy attempting to sleep. All of them have big frameless rucksacks, khaki shorts, dirty T-shirts, heavy leather boots with their socks rolled over the top and plastic bottles of mineral water in their hands; even the Dutchman who is trying to sleep clutches a bottle.

'Africa – have you been there much?'

It is the girl at my side.

'A bit.'

'Kilimanjaro?'

'The mountain? No.'

'I went up with Kevin from Birmingham and Sarah from Leeds and Jean Luc from Liège, or Lüttich as we say, and Federico from Milan, and Dorothea over there, that was before she had her breast operation, I mean, who would want to lug two tons of silicon to the top of a mountain five thousand, eight hundred and ninety-five metres high, and she could hardly have asked the bearers for help with that, we paid four hundred dollars each for the trip, it took five days with four overnights, and all the huts were full so we had to sleep in tents; one night I had Jean Luc on one side of me and Federico on the other, two pairs of hands at once; we had three bearers with us, carrying two bags each, and one leader, and a couple of catering people to make the meals and they carried everything they needed themselves, we took it pretty easily because everyone we met said how important it was to acclimatize yourself, I got a bit of a headache and felt nauseous, but that was all, and you expect something if you're climbing as high as that, I mean, well, five thousand, eight hundred and ninety-five metres is five thousand, eight hundred and ninety-five metres after all, and at the top the leader and the bearers and the catering people started to haggle about their tips, but we'd read in the Lonely Planet guide that it was important to make it clear there wouldn't be any tips till the end of the expedition, and we had made that very clear, at the end, OK, and yet they still tried to argue for a tip at the summit, threatened to dump us and our bags up there if we didn't give them anything; my God, we had to threaten them that we'd complain to the tour operators before we could persuade them to bring us down again, and then they were angry when we gave them the tip, thirty dollars from each of us to be shared out, just what it says in the Lonely Planet, but they were still angry.'

She takes a breath, lights a cigarette, has a drink from her bottle of water, pushes a lock of hair back behind her ear. In the clear morning light I can see she is wearing mascara and lipstick. Her intonation rises at the end of her sentences, making her sound pleasingly open.

'When I've done this I'll have all the four classics.'

'Kilimanjaro and Cuzco?'

'Sahara and safari.'

She moves up closer.

'I was at a friend's house once who had framed all her Lonely Planet book jackets, she said it helped her when the alarm clock went off in the mornings because she could sit down at the breakfast table and eat her muesli and remember that she had once been something other than a nurse and girlfriend of someone who hardly ever rang, she had once been a backpacker, for a whole six months.'

This last she says in a voice midway between dream and tears.

'How were your other two classics?'

'In trucks, like this one, but covered. One week in the Sahara, one week on safari.'

'How many of you were there?'

'Eighteen the first week, twelve the second. Plus caterers and drivers.'

I shut my eyes and see them before me. I have seen them driving past many times, young faces at the windows of converted trucks, on their way to see big game in the bush and listen to the silence of the desert.

'What's your situation at home?'

For a moment it seems as if she hasn't heard the question, or is searching for an answer and doesn't like what she finds. Then she takes a swig of water.

'I sent an e-mail to my father and said I was pregnant. He told me just to get on with it.'

She looks at me and laughs. Her upper arm is touching mine and she is running her fingers over my bracelet. 'There's light coming from it. Can you see it?'

We are leaning against a rock, using our rucksacks as side supports. Her hair is coming loose from its clasp and falling forward, making her look older. The others are sitting a few metres away, two of them alone, three in a group; the guide and bearers are nowhere to be seen. Everyone is on mescalin, I try to dissuade them, but can't get through to them: their contempt for adults is too great.

We've been walking all day, the truck set us down at the foot of a dense green hill with four other loads of back-packers. Five guides and twelve bearers of mixed Indian blood arrived to lead us in groups into the forest and up over the hill, after first collecting their money, half now, the rest in the morning, plus any little extra you might think the trip was worth, *gracias*. We stopped at an outcrop and had the temple ruins pointed out to us, the Temple of the Sun and the Convent of the Sun Virgin over there, the Temple of the Moon there, of the Stars there, of Thunder there, at the far end, and the American backpacker saw a railway track and asked whether it was the line to the Pacific, and the guide said no, that's over there, this one goes to Lake Titicaca, and on we go in columns up the steep broad path with its thick green foliage like a roof over our heads and humid air and few words, the trek starts at three-and-a-half thousand metres and we are still climbing; the choice is between moving or talking, except for the guide, who keeps stopping at regular intervals to turn round and hold a cassette player up in the air to let us listen to two minutes of concise introduction to the history of the Incas.

We arrive at our final destination one hour before sundown, the guide raises his hand to get everyone's attention, announcing. 'This is the Temple of the Fifth Dimension,' and a sigh goes up from the assembled flock.

We pitch camp and I attempt a sketch of the crumbling

steps and altars, and I think that if this is true, then mankind once not only saw existence in a different way but also built a temple to that way of seeing things; and when I have finished thinking about that I look over at the backpackers and realize what they are up to. I put my notebook and pencil in my pocket and go over to try to talk them out of it.

'Can you see the light?'

She is leaning up against me, her German accent more pronounced, her head drooping on to my shoulder. She is pointing with sudden excitement at the brown alpenstock she has stuck in the ground by the rucksack and the tent.

'Where did you get that?'

'The pawnbroker behind the railway station.'

'Did you all hire your sticks there?'

'Yes.'

'Why?'

'The pawnbroker is an old Austrian Jew. The sticks are from Jews who were sent to concentration camps. They had to leave everything behind. Even their sticks.'

'Why do you all walk with alpenstocks from European Jews here?'

'Haven't you heard the legend?'

'No.'

She tries to take her eyes off the stick for a moment but can't; instead she puts her head against mine and whispers as she continues to stare at it.

'When you bring the relics of one chosen people to the relics of another, you create an energy that's strong enough to release the fifth dimension. You unite the power from the people of God with the power from the people of the Sun, and the stick is the sign. If your stick starts to glow, you'll be admitted to the fifth dimension.

Some say it happens to one in a hundred, some say one in a thousand, but regardless of that, one is me, really, really me.'

A sound emanates from her as if she is humming as she speaks. I look at the stick and there is no mistake, green light is seeping out of the cracks in it, green light and yellow smoke. She tries to get up to go over to it, but I hold her down.

'Leave it.'

'But it's the fifth dimension.'

'It's not the stick that's the fifth dimension, it's your state of consciousness. The stick is just a sign. When you see a light during a mescalin trip, it's usually a sign that you're in place.'

'In place where?'

'In your place in existence. You have to find that before you can search for the fifth dimension.'

'I think I've found it.'

'What can you see?'

'I can see —'

She manages no more before she disappears. I keep my arm round her shoulders while she sits staring wide-eyed at the stick for three hours. I glance at the three backpackers sitting in a group, also in a trance, to make sure they have physical contact, and at the two sitting on their own, anxious about them.

Later, when she is lying with her head across my lap and one hand on my knee and her blond hair falling over her face so that I can't see the tears but only hear them, I ask her as gently as I can, 'What did you see?'

The silence is so protracted that I think she hasn't heard me, or can't manage an answer, isn't capable of one.

'My father.'

'What happened?'

172

'I was the sun rising above a temple, enormous and glowing white.'

'And?'

'He didn't see me.'

She sleeps for several hours and I watch over her, only leaving her when I check on the other five sleeping figures or write a bit or doze. On the way back down to the truck I ask cautiously, 'You guys who saw your sticks light up, are you going to return them to the pawnbroker?'

'Are you mad? We'd give anything to be able to take them home with us. Imagine having it on your wall. It's a bit different from book covers.'

'Anything?'

'Anything.'

She gives me a quick glance as she says it.

After accompanying the six backpackers to the hotel, I collect up five of the sticks to return them to the pawn-broker. On the way I go to an Internet café, pay for a connection, search the net for a while, send and receive a couple of e-mails and make some long-distance telephone calls. Then I gather up the sticks and go on to the pawnbroker.

The shop is almost a parody of itself, with piles of silverware in an old glass display counter, bags and clothes hanging from the ceiling, porcelain, books and statuettes on shelves round the walls. An elderly Indian dozes on a stool in one corner, the pawnbroker himself is leaning on the glass counter reading a news-paper. He is wearing a threadbare jacket and trousers, a waistcoat and collarless white shirt and a white Jewish skullcap. The Indian wakes up as the door opens and the bell above it tinkles, and peers through narrowed eyes at me and the five sticks. The pawnbroker doesn't look up.

I use one of the sticks to push the skullcap off the pawnbroker's head.

'What are you doing? Have you no respect for anyone's religion?'

The pawnbroker howls with rage as he throws aside his paper and bends down to retrieve the skullcap. I strike him across the back with one of the sticks, a short, sharp blow. The pawnbroker jerks upwards and hits his head on a leather bag. The old Indian can barely suppress a grin.

'What sort of ampoules do you use?'

The Indian runs to the door, puts two fingers to his mouth and whistles. A cobbler on the other side of the street raises his eyes from his workbench, a taxi driver sits up in the seat he has been sleeping in, a café owner dries his hands on a towel.

'Is it the altitude that perforates them, or have you worked out how long it takes to get to the temple and put some slow-acting corrosive substance in them?'

I slam the five sticks down on the counter with a crash, lean over and grab the pawnbroker by the lapels. Agitated cries from the doorway, where the cobbler and the taxi driver and the café owner are beckoning more people over. I pull the pawnbroker across the counter until our faces are almost touching:

'This is the last time you hire out sticks. You and I are going to take all the sticks you have, the ones already hollowed out and the ones that are not, and we're going out to the back yard to burn them.'

'You arrogant Aryan lout! What right have you to tell me what to do? Have you no respect for the sufferings of my people?'

The pawnbroker has finally found his voice. It is thick, as if full of something else besides anger.

'You're no Jew, you're a Kosovo Albanian. Look at this.'

I show a print-out from an Interpol web page with his picture on it. The pawnbroker goes pale. In the doorway the onlookers become increasingly vociferous.

'What sort of gas do you use to get both light and smoke? Chlorine?'

I start heaving the pawnbroker up, first over the glass counter, then up into the clothes and bags hanging from the ceiling. The audience by the door claps and chuckles. 'Do you use chlorine?' I yell louder. 'Do you use chlorine?' even louder. The spectators shout out into the street, 'Come and see this!' and the pawnbroker's head vanishes among three bags and a lady's grey coat. 'Do you use chlorine?' screaming now, lowering the pawnbroker but maintaining my grasp on jacket and shirt with one hand while taking a new grip on the knee of his trousers so that he is lying horizontally. One of the people in the doorway starts banging on a drum and another bursts into song. I sweep a shelf clear with the pawnbroker's head and shove him on to it, first his body, then his limbs. Next I pick up a roll of brown sticky tape from the counter and tear off four lengths that I stick over the shelves like the bars of a cage. The singing and drumming grow louder, the spectators are laughing and dancing. They step aside to let me through when I come towards them; a woman touches my arm as I pass her on my way out to the street. I turn and give her some money and ask her to burn the sticks, and she nods and touches me again. The elderly Indian pushes across and takes my hand as if to thank me, and I smile and say, 'Tell him the whole story is on hold on the net, and it will go out if anything happens to me and I don't put a stop on it every five hours.' Then I go off up the street, leaving the spectators in the doorway relishing the noises issuing from the shelf behind the bars of sticky tape.

A FRESH START

S he was standing at the window when I came in, which surprised me; she rarely stood still anywhere. The room was dark and she was silhouetted against a deep crimson sunset. I closed the door behind me and tapped with two fingers on the door frame.

'Hi.'

She turned, came across the room and put her arms round me, pressing her face against my chest for a few moments before stepping back to scrutinize me.

'Have you been all right?'

'Have you?'

She didn't reply, just took me by the arm and led me out to the kitchen.

'Hungry?'

'Are you?'

She got vegetables from one cupboard, pasta from another, she rattled casseroles and knives and whisks and drawers until I could barely hear the voice hovering over the room, the small, thin voice that sings whenever life stops and stands still and you know that nothing will ever be the same again. She poured me a drink and set me to work slicing onions.

'Tell me what you've been up to.'

The voice hovering over the room became weaker, almost disappeared, and I knew we could save ourselves whenever we wanted, that we could go on. For a brief moment life had lain wide open before us and the voice above had sung; now it was nearly over.

'I saw a remarkable theatre production.'

The voice above became thinner, more fearful.

'*Romeo and Juliet*. In Mong La.'

The voice was reduced to a whisper.

'What was remarkable about it?'

'All the actors stood at a window with their backs to the auditorium throughout the whole performance.'

A short screech from above, a gust of wind through the room, my words swirled around her and she buckled under their onslaught.

'It must have been difficult to hear what they were saying.'

'Yes, it was, but I knew the words.'

She filled a casserole with water, added some broccoli, lit the gas and put it on. Then she swung round, folded her arms and asked, 'And my words, do you know them?'

'No. But now that you're facing me it's easier to hear them.'

She looked hard at me, at my clothes, my shoulders, my face, my eyes; then turned away with a sad smile.

'Iraq has offered us unlimited aid, economic, military and political, if we call our republic Islamic.'

'And?'

'The Central Committee is divided.'

I lowered my eyes, dared not meet hers; picked up the knife and went on cutting the onions, the Central Committee is divided, chop, chop, chop, those in favour of the Iraqi offer we'll chop up and put here, those against we'll chop up and put there, that's where you can go, chop, chop, chop, once upon a time there was a Central Committee and the knife slipped and made a little nick in my index finger as she threw herself on my back, knocking me into the kitchen unit, tore the knife from my grasp, seized both my hands and banged them against the doors of the wall cabinet, banged and banged and banged so that everything inside shook. Then she held my arms and put them round me, mine and her own, and clung tight.

'Has it occurred to you that you live in a dream? Your journeys are dreams, the conversations you describe are dreams, even the wars you report on are dreams, you can change them with a stroke of your pen. But we are living in reality, the Iraqis have offered us unlimited support if we call ourselves an Islamic republic, and the Central Committee is divided.'

She squeezed me tighter, I could feel the full length of her body, she put her lips to my neck and whispered, 'We need schools, we need hospitals, we need roads; we need a modern defence system, we need political support.'

'But you also need dreams.'

The voice came back later on, taking me by surprise. It only came when life stopped and stood still, but now life was not standing still, now it was floating on a calm wide river of soft skin. I could hear the voice out in the kitchen, like a hymn, bright and beautiful; I could see a soldier kneeling bareheaded among many soldiers; all the others had helmets on. The bareheaded one looked up and sang, and the song was a dream, an expression of hope.

'What is it?'

She raised her head from the pillow to peer at me.

'I don't know. I just twitched.'

The song had come nearer, the bareheaded soldier must be standing right outside the bedroom with all the other soldiers. I could hear their silence.

She pulled me to her. The taste of tears and silk, the song of a bareheaded soldier and the darkness slowly starting to spin.

'You've been crying.'

She nodded.

'Yes, I've been crying. And when you write about this one day, when one day you write about this as well, put in that you did not ask why.'

A hum, it was the darkness spinning faster.

She lifted my arm, stroked my armpit, blew into it gently, touched it with her lips.

'And say I just did this when you write, so that everyone who reads it will know who I am, what race I belong to, what culture I come from. Put in that I am whispering this to you, not shouting it, not screaming it, not beating it into you, I'm whispering it: you're not asking why because you're no longer participating.'

Out of the darkness came a cry and the sound of running feet.

'When you write about that, you won't even try to defend yourself, you'll reproduce what I'm saying, word for word, without comment.'

She stretched up and let her lips tickle my cheeks, first the left and then the right.

'If I hadn't done that, you wouldn't even have mentioned your own tears, they wouldn't have existed.'

She pressed up closer behind my back and put her arms around me, held my head to her shoulder.

Isabelle Eberhardt was standing in front of us; she had climbed out of the spinning darkness and was standing at the foot of the bed, not half turned away this time but with her gaze fixed on the woman behind me. By her side stood a Tibetan monk.

'What did you want her for?'

Her voice was just by my ear. I put my hands on her wrists.

'To show you that trying to forget – oblivion – is flight.'

'And the monk?'

182

I stroked her arms, ran my fingers up to her elbows and down again, up again and down again. She hugged me tighter.

'What about the monk?'

The bareheaded soldier was in the room now, I could hear him there somewhere, his song increasing in volume with the darkness, rising and falling, rising and falling; the other soldiers had taken up position in a circle around the darkness and were giving it impetus, pushing it as it passed to provide a quick boost and speed it on its way.

'Did you want to show me that there's something that lasts, something that remains firm?'

'Something of that nature.'

She undressed behind me and pulled off my clothes.

'It's not me who needs to know that something lasts, it's you.'

Strong hands and a hint of nutmeg.

'I know this could last, I know we could last. It's you who doesn't know, or doesn't want to know.'

She turned me round and rubbed her nose against mine as she looked me in the eyes.

'What did you want all the others for?'

They were leaping down from the carousel darkness as she spoke, holding on to the song of the bareheaded soldier and leaping down; first the pawnbroker, then the two women from the sperm bank. The pawnbroker invited them to dance and they smiled their acceptance and offered their hands, which he kissed gallantly, then he danced with light little steps around and between them. Captain Hawthorne was looking on grumpily, clapping the beat, and behind him the kebab seller was opening the shutters of his hut against a background rattle of vacuum pumps knocking together. From a corner of the room the editor observed anxiously.

'The dreams of oblivion, the body, freedom, immortality,

power, riches, a fresh start, peace, are they all there now? Can you see them?'

She took my head in her hands again and tilted it back.

'Are they there?'

'Yes.'

'Why do you think you can see them and I can't?'

The hum from the darkness was increasing to a thunderous roar, and I could hear cries.

'Because you have lost them?'

'Or because you have invented them?'

As her young nation gradually and uncertainly raised itself, first to its knees and then to its feet, I could see it begin to look about for an identity. Some wanted the king back, some wanted a republic, but most, it seemed, just wanted to cleanse themselves of the shame and humiliation of the years of occupation.

She was active at this stage too. On Fridays and at weekends she travelled the country in a truck with other volunteers holding political meetings, in villages, at markets, outside mosques and churches. They rolled into people's daily lives without warning, with their white banners and slogans on placards and microphones and loudspeakers on the back of the truck. '*We are a nation*,' she shouted through the shrill loudspeaker, and people stared at her and, I imagined, asked one another what a nation was. We know what a tribe is and we know what a clan is, but a nation? Is it a place where women go about dressed like her, in olive-green military trousers and white T-shirts? And they looked at her hips, their contour visible under her trousers, and whispered don't those hips belong to a man, is a nation a place where men let their women show their hips to everyone? '*We are a nation*,' she cried, and people crowded round the truck and stared at her, and a few days later another truck arrived full of young Muslim boys in white headbands.

'*Our world is Islam,*' they cried. 'We must all rid ourselves of the leprous sores the West has infected us with,' and they handed out cassette tapes of the Imam's speeches until the police came and moved them on.

A few days later came a truck full of Christian men.

'*We are the light in the Islamic darkness,*' they cried. '*Be a light unto yourselves.*' And they handed out little paper stars bearing biblical quotations until the police came and moved them on.

Then the Party truck was back again.

'*We want democracy,*' she said, her bare brown arms radiant against her white T-shirt, and they asked what democracy was, and she said it was a place where people chose their leader themselves, and they asked what would happen then, people were likely to choose just about anything, and she replied, 'We shall keep it all under strict supervision,' and with those words she put the plough into untilled soil, and with those words the people who came after her in the next truck also sowed, *veleyat-e faqih,* we shall keep everything under strict supervision.

Veleyat-e faqih.

The words were whispered in prayer with forehead and nose to the ground, muttered at washbasins outside mosques, sometimes shouted on the streets, suddenly, in anger, and then running steps fading into the distance.

Veleyat-e faqih. For the country's Muslims it represented a longing, a dream of finally being able to feel themselves whole individuals again. With *veleyat-e faqih* as a form of state the country would be led by someone well versed in the Scriptures, and candidates for elections would have to pass through a religious filter; *veleyat-e faqih,* a religious democracy that would eventually be able to purge the country, remove the shame and wipe away all trace of foreign occupation.

Veleyat-e faqih.

The words were spat in the sewer, declaimed from pulpits, blared through loudspeakers.

Veleyat-e faqih. For the Christians of the country it was a constant anxiety, a nightmare slowly eroding their hopes for reform, for a modern life. With *veleyat-e faqih* as a form of state, democracy for them would be a pseudo-democracy, supervised and controlled by the Muslim priesthood.

And yet there was an ambiguity in both the Christians' and the Muslims' attitude to *veleyat-e faqih*. The country's Christian Church was related to an authoritarian, dogmatic branch of Christianity, and the bishops could not agree on which was the greater evil, a godless or an Islamic regime; Islam was a Mosaic religion after all. For Muslims the question was more complex; the priests wanted *veleyat-e faqih*, wanted the power to purge, but there was disquiet among the Muslim community. Few would put it into words, few talked about it, but in the tea-stalls on the marketplace Muslims would sometimes look at their Christian neighbours doubtfully, as if they were afraid of what the relationship between them might be under *veleyat-e faqih*.

When I came back from the truck meetings he listened to me with an attentive if sometimes pensive air. He would put an occasional question, but mostly he just sat and listened and watched me, creating a reticence between us that had not existed before, a silent discontinuity between what I was telling him and what he appeared to be thinking. I spoke of land reform, he asked about corn seed and tools; I spoke about prohibiting dowries, he asked about the bride's and family's honour; I advocated that all property should belong to the state, he asked whether the tribe's property was not the tribe's most significant strength; but he didn't pursue matters further, he listened to the answer and waited for me to continue.

Sometimes he was not there when I returned. We had been living together long enough for me not to be worried. He based himself at my place every other month and I was used to his going off to appointments and didn't like to think of him sitting alone in the apartment while I was away. But sometimes I was uneasy when I came home to an empty house, and that would be when he had left a note to say he was at the market. He always left a note. When it said he was at the market I would lock the verandah door and all the windows and smear scorpion-poison unguent on the window frames and doorstep, knowing that he was at the market behind the market, where they sold blood and amulets, and I didn't want to let in what he might bring home with him from there. Once a neighbour unexpectedly appeared while I was smearing the keyhole of the door to the stairs, and I had to hide the pot of unguent hurriedly behind my back.

He travelled even in the months he was living with me, but for shorter journeys than usual. A fax might arrive from his office one day, he would be off the next morning, and back a week later, a much quieter man. For me the war was over; for him it still continued, but elsewhere. Sometimes he was the only reporter, sometimes he travelled with others, and he seemed content with either.

———

Angry and a bit drunk. Two hopelessly white reporters, angry and a bit drunk. We were sitting under a fig tree in a remote corner of the globe, an African province where distances are measured in days and everywhere is a week away. We had been

187

walking all day past rows of starving children, counting; one in ten had no chance of survival. We had talked to young people who were digging bomb shelters a metre deep as protection against splinter bombs that killed everything within a five-hundred-metre radius. We had flown in with the first food supplies, in the big white bird that was seen by all, and four days later there were still streams of desperate people pouring in.

We were going to spend the night beneath the fig tree, a cool canopy in the baking white heat. My friend had set up the satellite telephone and had to take it down again in impotent fury: four European tourists had been hacked to pieces by the Rwandan Hutu militia; they were this week's story from the jungle and there was no space for us.

'Shit awful tabloids.'

He was shouting.

'Please, not the tabloid lecture. Not tonight. Tonight I think we should share the rest of this flask while we listen to the singing and the drums over there, and for each capful we drink we can be sure that one person dies in Kabul, and that's distressing to think of, but there's a lot of distress and evil in the world, and here we sit.

'You've become such a cynic.'

'And please, not your cynic lecture, promise me you won't give me your cynic lecture.'

'Not even the abridged version?'

'If you absolutely must.'

'To hell with the tabloids!'

He bellowed it at the top of his voice, standing with his hands cupped like a megaphone in front of his mouth; his scream disappeared on outstretched wings over four million square kilometres of sundrenched plains; not savannah, that would be too fertile, but dry, sandy, dusty plains.

'Go on.'

He turned towards me, planted one hand on his hip and

pointed at me with the other, trembling with rage and indignation.

'I've covered this continent for more than ten years and seen most things, but I've never met anyone as cynical as you.'

His voice quivered with suppressed fury.

'You've met me a few times. Cheers.'

'Cheers.'

His hand was shaking as he took the cap of brandy.

'Is that better?'

'A bit.'

We sat with our backs against the tree trunk and the flask between us. The singing stopped, the drums were mute for increasingly lengthy periods, the fires were dying down. I looked up at the sky, full of stars, and something opened in me, like a hatch. I knew I was going to write 'A quilt of stars was drawn over the end of the world,' and already felt ashamed.

He began to talk. He took his time, searching for the right words.

'Do you remember when we started on this?'

'It was here, but a bit further south.'

'East.'

'Southeast?'

'OK. We were both different then, not young, not idealists, but different. Can you remember how we were? With neckerchiefs and notebooks? You always used to let me go first in case of landmines. That was when you began walking the same way as me, do you remember that?'

'Up till then I didn't have any particular way of walking.'

'Neither of us was naive, we had served enough time. We knew there was no automatic connection between a famine warning and the world coming to the rescue. But we also knew there was a conscience out there, and that our task, our duty, was to keep prodding at that conscience for as long as the crisis continued.'

He waved his arm in a wide arc towards the darkened landscape with its dying fires and gurgling coughs.

'It's still basically the same, but there's one big difference from those days.'

I took a swig of the brandy, leaned my head back and closed my eyes. I knew what was coming.

'In those days we believed there was a limit for African famine disasters, that they could be arrested. Now we know that's not so, that these famine disasters are part of the Africans' adaptation to nature and climate. They'll go on for ever. And so the question remaining is how long you and I should subject ourselves to them.'

For some time neither of us said anything. I could hear a trap being set, hear the spring being tensioned.

'I've read what you wrote about infidelity.'

He spoke quietly, not looking at me.

' "The real infidelity is knowing that the other person's image of you is not a true one any more, but saying nothing." Is that still your opinion?'

Trap, trap.

'Yes.'

'Our readers trust us; if we say there's famine in a particular region, then there's famine there. And if we don't say there's famine there, then there isn't. Is that correct?'

Clunk.

'Yes.'

We sat in thought for a while. He rolled a cigarette and lit it.

'Why are you keeping quiet about the situation?'

He still did not look at me.

'Because I still don't know enough.'

'Good try. Why are you keeping quiet?'

'Because I'll lose her the day I write about it.'

'When have you ever let that kind of thing deter you?'

'Now.'

190

He let it drop and we unpacked our sleeping bags and lay down. I put one arm over my eyes and thought to myself that if I went on keeping quiet I would lose her anyway, and which would be worse?

I started on a six-line introduction, decided that it had to include the phrases political uniformity, strict supervision and authoritarian regime, composed some sentences to a little staccato sentence tune, the way an alarm sounds, and felt something fall into place. My friend brought me back just as I was drifting off to sleep.

'What does she mean to you?'

'She has given me life.'

He was silent for a moment, long enough for me to know what he was going to say.

'How sad.'

———

One day he had a visit from two men from the Party. I was on the verandah when they came and I watched the official black car from the minute it appeared at the top of the street. I watched it park in front of my house, watched the chauffeur get out and open the rear doors, first one side and then the other, and watched the two men in dark suits heave themselves rather stiffly out of the car and disappear into the doorway. I stayed on the verandah until I heard that it was my doorbell they were ringing.

They were from the Ministry of Information, both in their late thirties, neither seeming to have had battle experience, at least neither gave the veterans' greeting when I opened the door, they just strode past me and into the living room. I drew up two chairs and they sat down, one of them placing a document wallet on his knees. I asked whether they wanted anything to drink and they declined, the one with the papers taking out a bundle of newspaper cuttings and spreading them on the table. They were all in Italian.

'Were these written by the man you're living with?'

I went closer to the table and inspected the cuttings, they were for the most part background articles and reportage, each covering a whole page, all on my country: on the political situation, economic and social developments.

'Why do you ask? His name is at the top of every one of them.'

'We just wanted to confirm it. Have you read them?'

'Is this an interrogation?'

'No. But we can call you in to the Ministry if you'd prefer. We had in mind a softer approach.'

I gazed at him, he was rather plump and wore gold-rimmed spectacles.

'He says he doesn't want to show his articles to me because he doesn't want to see me as a hostage.'

The man with the gold-rimmed spectacles looked surprised, as if he didn't entirely understand.

'If he had shown it to you and you had discovered that he had written something that was quite obviously wrong, what would you have done?'

'I would have told him.'

'And then?'

'He would have been pleased that I had drawn it to his attention.'

'And if it hadn't concerned facts, but opinions?'

'His?'

'Yes.'

'Then I would have said what I thought.'

'Would he have sent it in to the newspaper anyway?'

'It's his name at the head of it.'

There was a pause. The man in the gold-rimmed spectacles

was studying his nails, the one with the document wallet was beginning to get annoyed.

'Can you tell me why you're here?'

'We've come to tell you that what he's writing is no longer of service to us. And there is some doubt in the Ministry about whether a foreign correspondent of a hostile disposition has any place in this country.'

I stared from one to the other and then stood up and went out on to the verandah, grasping the rail with both hands and biting my lip.

I could hear the two of them talking in the room, and down in the street I could see him approaching. He was walking lightly, almost dancing. I stayed where I was on the verandah, heard him let himself in, greet the two men from the Ministry, listen to what they had to say. I closed my eyes, I heard him ask if they would be kind enough to show him what was actually wrong in the articles he had written, and I listened to the painful silence that followed. I heard the men from the Ministry propose, in their circumspect phraseology, that from now on they should see what he had written before he sent it, and I opened my eyes and looked straight at him as he said no, he was sorry he couldn't, and he said nothing else before opening the door for them and wishing them a good trip back to the Ministry, and I smiled and went in to him, and as I stood holding him I felt a dream coming from him, the dream of a fresh start, and I whispered, 'This time I'll come too.'

October 12th

The cover of my diary was brown leather, the same colour as my skin. It had a clasp with a little brass lock. The first thing I did when I bought it was to write his name in it and lock it. I could hear him shouting from within the pages when I turned the miniature key. I remembered smiling and squeezing the diary between my fingers. I had also bought a camera for this trip, a Polaroid, which was more expensive than a normal one, but I wanted to have the pictures immediately, not in a week or a month, when they had already become memories. The same applied to the diary: when I wrote in it I always did so on the day itself, while it was still now, not then. I planned to put the photographs of him between the pages, in various places.

Punta Porvenir was like most Argentinian bus stations: the buses never arrived and they never left; they stood with their engines idling outside the bus station while the same goods were loaded on and off amidst much clamour and confusion. Beside the newspaper kiosk four Indians sat drinking themselves into a stupor, by the ticket-office window were two men wearing white suits and gold watches. It was hot and the sheets of corrugated iron that formed the roof were turning the bus station into an oven. One of the men in white suits glanced at me from time to time, but I didn't catch his eye. He could see I was from a different culture, which was enough to awaken the instinct, and that irritated me.

Punta Porvenir, Patagonia, the end of the world. What was I doing here?

Punta Porvenir, Patagonia, the end of the world, for centuries a goal for people who had burnt all their bridges: anarchists, dreamers, outlaws, exiles and adventurers, a real spectrum of people at the foot of the South American continent, right at the bottom, the furthest away it was possible to get.

Punta Porvenir, Patagonia, the end of the world. What was I doing here?

I ate some dried fruit and watched him as he came walking along. The same green metal-framed rucksack, the same grey shirt with the two breast pockets, the same black trousers.

Punta Porvenir, Patagonia, and his arms around me. The

walls of the bus station were painted in a subdued ochre colour with azure-blue doors, and out on the square in front of the bus station there was something reminiscent of an acacia tree. We walked past it and down the main street, and it felt as if there had never been anything except this: arriving in a new place.

October 20th
He was having nightmares again. I was woken by his restlessness and talking in his sleep, shouting almost. It was impossible to make out what he was saying, I wasn't even sure what language it was, but it was obvious he was afraid. I tried to put my hand on his shoulder, but he edged away. I tried to talk to him, to wake him, but it seemed as if he couldn't manage to extricate himself from what he was in. Eventually he became calmer, or at least quieter. I asked him about it at breakfast.

'Nightmares?'
'Yes.'
'Have they come back?'
'Yes. And you?'
'The same.'
'What are you dreaming now?'
So he wanted me to talk.
'In the most frequent one I'm sitting on the back of a truck with green hills all around, the road winding between them, a white dusty gravel road bordered by willow trees whose branches I can touch as we pass underneath. The sunlight is shining through the foliage in rapid flickers, making everything look like a film, a jerky film running at slow speed.'
'Then I know where you are, we were there together. Am I with you in the dream?'
'Sometimes. Sometimes you're standing by me with your kerchief tied over your nose and mouth, at other times you

suddenly appear at the side of the road waiting; neither of us says anything when the truck stops and you climb aboard: it's as if there are no words any more.'

'And then?'

'I hear a noise behind me, above the roar of the engine, and turn round: there's a white horse galloping after the truck, with flared nostrils and foam at its muzzle. The rider is carrying something; he yells at the horse to make it gallop faster, the truck comes to a hill and changes gear, slows down, the horse overtakes it, drenched with sweat. The rider is black and naked, the black and white contrast against the green hills and the flashing glints of sunlight are a splendid sight.'

'And what is he carrying?'

'A child. It's bleeding, the blood streaming out behind it like a ribbon, extending further than I can see, a thin, red stream of blood suspended above a dusty white gravel road, as if someone had taken a photograph of the road and drawn in the red ribbon with a coloured pencil. The child looks round at me as it passes and its face gradually dissolves and disappears; eyes and nose and mouth and chin melt into shadow, and the only thing I can make out in the shadow is the eyes, still focused on me, from further and further away.'

'And then?'

'And then nothing.'

We sat in silence for a while.

'And what about you?'

'I hear a voice. And see something moving. The voice belongs to an officer; I think we may be in a prison. He says I'm going to be executed in three days' time and I'm desperately trying to get it postponed, to gain time.'

'And what is it that's moving?'

'Something heading towards me at breakneck speed, something shining, getting closer and closer each time.'

'What is it?'

'I don't know. And I don't know whether I'm afraid or just feel sorrowful, don't even know whether it's myself or another person I'm afraid or sorry for. There's another person there with me.'

I waited, but nothing else was forthcoming. He looked as if he was deep in thought, and I let him alone. We had talked before well into the night, in war zones, but this was different, this was different from the images we bore within ourselves. I knew he would come back to my dream, and he knew that I would come back to his. We had the remainder of the trip ahead of us, maybe even longer.

October 24th

Another restless night. I reached out and felt his forehead: it was hot. I stroked his cheek: it was wet. I think someone was communicating with him, far, far away and deep, deep down.

October 25th

Malaria. It seemed as if he was withdrawing into the fever and disappearing, letting the fever act as a barrier between himself and others. I had never seen him so defenceless. I sat outside drinking coffee on the verandah and reading Marxist theory. The gauchos tried to make conversation with me.

November 7th

We were sitting looking at my photographs from Tierra del Fuego, the land of fire. One of them was of two men holding a horse, handsome, proud men with long glistening hair. It was not that which captured the attention but an old man on a bench in the background. His eyes were magnetic, the light reflected in them in a way that gave them depth, opening them up so that you could see right into them, a long way in, and discern many things: cares, hopes, despair, dreams. His face had

a network of wrinkles around the eyes, wrinkles either pointing to the eyes or growing out from them, I couldn't decide
which. He was wearing a red kerchief round his neck, his grey
hair was combed straight back, with either water or hair cream.
He was stooped and was leaning on a stick, but at the same time
there seemed to be a great strength in him.

November 13th

There was something about images I found disquieting. He
had visual memories of me from the war front, and I had visual
memories of him, but not of myself; I only had visual
memories of war, not of myself in war; yet I knew he went
in and out of his stories as he wrote, even for newspapers, and
that enabled him to see himself in war, to analyse his own role.

November 18th

'What is the difference between describing something and
participating in it? Are they points at opposite ends of a scale?'

We were sitting on a bus full of Indians, small Indians with
plaited hair and hats and pipes, and he asked me what the
difference was between describing something and participating in it. Some of the Indians had their wives with them, but
most were travelling alone or with other men.

'Is it the case that those who describe have greater oppor-
tunities for manipulating reality than those who actually
participate? Don't both intervene in reality and change it?'

The driver was an Indian too, and he was playing Indian
music over the loudspeakers, shrill Indian music. The Indian
beside me kept trying to put his hand on my knee.

'The question of course is why we choose the reality we
choose, irrespective of whether we are describing it or
participating in it. We are given the chance to choose the
beautiful, the poetic, the inspiring, but some of us choose the
cruel, the frightful, the loathsome. Why?'

Outside the window the green pampas was gliding by, beyond the distant hills the sun was turning red, and a condor was sailing towards the horizon on outstretched wings. I asked, 'Are you sure it's a question of choice?'

'Yes, but on the other hand we must be careful about questioning too much. Aristotle would have called us ill-mannered; we have to stop somewhere or we end up asking why there is anything instead of nothing.'

Oh God, he was far away now.

When the bus continued its journey without us we were left standing on an endless green plain. That was one of the things I liked about him, he got off buses in places where no one else would.

He pointed.

'We can go that way.'

'It's an attractive horizon.'

'Or that way.'

'A village – tiny, but a village nevertheless.'

'With lemonade for you and grappa for me.'

He picked up his rucksack and took my arm.

'Come on, let's go.'

That was another thing I liked about him, grappa. He asked for grappa everywhere on his travels. He never got it, but he still went on asking.

'If someone were to take a picture of us now, what would it show?'

He cupped his hands to indicate a lens.

'Colour or black-and-white?'

'Colour.'

'Two travellers on an endless green plain.'

'Where are they going?'

'Towards a village. Yellow.'

'How are they walking?'

'With their arms round one another.'
'And with audio equipment, what would be heard?'
'Their footsteps.'
'What else?'
'A donkey.'
'What else?'
'Shots.'
'What sort of shots?'
'AK 47.'
'Where are the shots coming from?'
'The village.'
'Single shots or bursts of gunfire?'
'Both.'
'At long intervals?'
'No.'
'Mmm. Grappa and hand-to-hand combat.'
'Can you take over the story now?'

Captain Mendoza is not in a good mood. His lover has shaved herself without asking him, his son has started playing the violin again, and now he has two foreigners in his sights.

'Long live Patagonia! Let's face our future together! Patagonia for ever!'

It is the Governor on the radio, making an appeal to the people every other hour. There is general agreement that the appeals are going from bad to worse and that for this reason alone it is imperative to have some clarification of the military coup.

Captain Mendoza is sitting on the floor under the window in the police station, surrounded by trouser-seats and legs: his soldiers hanging out of the window defending their fatherland. Every time they open fire they howl, and the howls when they let off continuous bursts of gunfire are the worst, long-drawn-out and piercing, reminding him of his son's violin-playing. He can also hear shots and howls from outside, the bandits from the Patagonian Federal Army (PFA).

'Captain! They're shooting at the Venus de Milo!'

Captain Mendoza jumps up with a start. Enough is enough. He sticks his head out of the window and roars, 'You damned rabble! Leave the statue alone!'

A puff of plaster dust from the statue's breast. He can see the bandits in the house across the street, wearing red headbands and with three vertical stripes of white paint on each cheek. At the side of the house stands a group of men in black hats and frock coats, all with long black beards pinned into ringlets. They have one placard which says 'Kosher Republic King Kong', another saying 'King Kong Kosher' and a third saying 'Kosher King': they are unable to agree on anything beyond declaring their support for those who would declare Free Patagonia kosher.

On the other side of the house is a group of Welsh sheep farmers. They have no placards, they have just come to watch the day's exchange of gunfire, which makes good entertainment, and to see which side the Jews will choose, so that they will know which to choose themselves.

The PFA can be brutal, but they are much better than the Patagonian Anarchist League (PAL), who have recently adopted the irritating habit of throwing Molotov cocktails into the police-station yard, admittedly only miniature bottles of petrol that are easy to put out. The problem is that at the same time as filling the bottles, corking them with a rag, lighting them and throwing them, the anarchists are also downing the original contents, so that their aim becomes increasingly erratic during the course of the day. The previous week one had hit the Venus de Milo, and if there was one thing they had all agreed on at the tripartite talks held a fortnight earlier, it was that the statue in front of the police station should be spared. Signs, shutters, drainpipes and flagpoles, yes, and walls of course, well away from windows, but Venus de Milo, no, absolutely not: they are not barbarians.

The day's shooting match has been going on for barely an hour when the two foreigners arrive. Captain Mendoza doesn't know whether to laugh or cry – can't they be left to get on with anything in peace? Now that it is all going so well? Police troops had taken the police station on Monday, and that afternoon they are going to evacuate it and hand it over to the PFA; on Friday it will be the PFA's turn to bite the dust and surrender to the PAL, and on Monday the police will attack and drive out the PAL. That way all three can report back to their headquarters of their victory after a close-fought battle in Buen Tiempo, and next week the alliance season will be starting: first the police and PFA against PAL, then the police and PAL against PFA, then PAL and PFA against the police – are there any more combinations possible? The Baptist Sunday School teacher says there are two, but he won't elucidate.

Captain Mendoza glares at the foreigners in exasperation. It was Juan in the café who had phoned about them: they had been drinking coffee there before they walked into the battle; he recognized them as foreigners because he knew about such things.

With some reluctance Captain Mendoza has to admit that the woman is attractive, her back temptingly arched as she crawls on all fours; but as for the man behind her, he cannot find in him a single sympathetic trait, even his notebook is unsympathetic and he is holding it in his teeth by its spiral binding as he crawls along. Any idiot can see that it ought to be held with its spiral binding outwards.

The foreigners have got halfway along the wall of the house and are equidistant between the Jews and the Welsh sheep farmers when the Captain gives the order to let off a salvo above their heads. The police troops obey enthusiastically; one of them sprays an arc of bullets from just in front of the woman to just behind the man, the others hammer their bullets into the house wall higher up, one taking the gutters. The two foreigners stop and huddle against the wall, the woman looking in the direction of the gunfire, the man pulling a pencil out of his left breast pocket.

'Jesus and Mary, what are we doing?'

The Captain hears himself scream in anger; the police troops stare at him in amazement.

'Jesus and Mary, what are you doing?'

It is Carlos on the telephone from the house across the street. The Captain can see him in the first-floor window, pointing an accusing finger at his red headband.

Captain Mendoza doesn't reply. His lover has shaved herself without asking him, his son has taken up the violin again, and now he has two foreigners in his sights. It isn't his day.

'The only way we can get rid of those two idiots is by stopping shooting, and then the war will be over. Then you will have won and we will have lost, and PAL won't even get a look in. What kind of ass are you?'

'Are you calling me an ass?'

'Yes I am.'

The Captain runs to the window with the telephone to his ear as he loosens the strap of his holster and draws his gun, leaning backwards the way he has seen it done in the movies, takes aim from the hip and fires two bullets into the window opposite at Carlos.

'Are you out of your mind?'

Carlos yells so loud that the Captain has to hold the receiver right away from his ear.

'No one calls me an ass and gets away with it.'

'I'll call you what I like.'

Carlos disappears from the window and reappears a few seconds later in the window above the Jews with a white loud-hailer in his hand. It crackles into life and Carlos shouts, 'On this great day of the revolution we wish to make an official announcement that Captain Manuel Mendoza is an ass, conceived of an ass, born of an ass!'

An agitated hubbub breaks out among the Jews. They begin gesticulating so violently that they nearly lose their narrow black hats, and the Captain empties his revolver at the man with the red headband and white warpaint and loud-hailer, but too late.

'We also wish to announce officially on this great day in the history of the revolution that the Captain's lover Fernanda Valdes has had herself shaved!'

The Captain leaps out of the window like a tiger and races across to the house opposite. 'How do you know that, you bastard?' And the loud-hailer screeches, 'I was the one who shaved her,' and the Jews explode in mirth and even the Welsh sheep farmers start jumping up and down. Captain Mendoza is yelling and loading his revolver as he runs, and he raises it above his head and lets off six shots into the air, stopping in front of the two foreigners and reloading as he roars at them, 'What the hell are you doing here? Can't you even let people make war in peace?'

'Ass!'

Carlos, with the loud-hailer, at the window directly above them. The Captain fires a shot, but again too late. He turns back to the foreigners.

'What right have you to meddle in other people's wars? Can't you see that you're wrecking everything?'

'Ass!'

Carlos again, with the loud-hailer, from a window a bit further away. The Captain runs towards him shooting as he goes, but just too late again. He stamps the ground in rage, close to tears, and fires the rest of his bullets into a metal water barrel under the drainpipe on the corner. The barrel rocks and splits and water spurts out.

'Ass!'

Carlos, with the loud-hailer, now in the window above the Welsh sheep farmers. Captain Mendoza takes aim and fires once more, fast enough this time, but click, click, click, empty. He roars in frustration, pulling out more bullets as he runs, one in, two in, three in, and he has his finger and thumb on the fourth when he trips and sprawls forward, clutching at the rim of the water barrel as he falls. It tilts towards him and in he goes head first, the barrel still half full of water, almost a metre deep, and he shrieks with pain as he hits the bottom. The Welsh sheep farmers watch the bubbles rising before both Captain and barrel roll over and all the water spills out, leaving the Captain sitting up in the barrel, just able to make out through the bullet holes in the side the two foreigners being hauled in through the windows of the first floor by the PFA. The bandits have thrown down ropes from two of the windows and the foreigners are clambering calmly up the wall. He can see the woman's breasts rising and falling beneath her T-shirt as she climbs, surprisingly full for a woman so slim, bigger than Fernanda's. The Captain bellows with rage at the thought of Fernanda, drumming on the water barrel with both hands, triggering his revolver and sending a bullet straight into the Venus de Milo in front of the police station.

The police troops barricaded behind the windows call excitedly to one another and start shooting at the statue too. If that is the way he wants it, they won't let him down; they fire with the hearty enjoyment with which men always shoot at statues of naked women, and the PFA on the other side of the street join in; after all, the following week is alliance week, and this is no bad start. When the Captain succeeds in extracting himself from the empty barrel, the first thing he sees is the concrete statue gradually disintegrating before his very eyes. The beautiful female body he has purchased on the market in Puerto Natales and brought here in a requisitioned truck has been reduced to fragments and dust, and something dies in him. He remembers reading that without the Venus de Milo the human race would be all the more wretched, and that is exactly how he feels now, insignificant and wretched. His lover has shaved without asking him and has not even done it herself; his son has taken up the violin again, two foreigners have ruined the war, Carlos has called him an ass in public, the Venus de Milo has gone, leaving only a bullet-riddled concrete plinth, and he is soaked to the skin. How much more wretched can you possibly get?

November 27th

'Was that what happened?'

We were sitting on white plastic chairs, he with a glass of wine, I with a cup of tea.

'We were both there.'

'But if I had written about it?'

'Then it would have been a different war.'

Right in front of us was a little arcaded church of colourless brick, lovingly constructed, like an embroidery, for use only on special occasions, finery for Sundays and festivals, but not for everyday use.

'What do you think I would have mentioned? A boy getting his hand shot off? The incredulity in his eyes when he saw the stump of his wrist pumping blood?'

'Maybe.'

He was being defensive.

'Or the scream of a woman finding her husband dead at the garden gate with his throat cut?'

'Maybe.'

'Do you think I would have included the way her scream gradually turned into sobbing, desperate, devastated, inconsolable sobbing?'

'Maybe.'

'Aren't you ever going to take off that red headband? Buen Tiempo is a while ago now.'

I dipped my napkin in his wine.

'Come here and I'll wash off your war paint.'

'The last PFA fighter?'

'Yes.'

It had been a long day, hot sun and very windy. I didn't know anything that could so transform a landscape as wind; it took all the colour out of it, until the landscape looked like the church in front of us, built by German Calvinists, in homage to a colourless life. The railway station was a little further down the street, a platform with three pillars and a roof and a low glass wall to protect against the wind. Two tracks crossed the flat pampas side by side, receding towards the far horizon and gradually converging until they became one. A goods wagon converted into living accommodation was parked on one of the tracks in the station, with a desolate, resigned air about it. Perhaps a train would come some time, but there would never be two, that was for sure. Perhaps a train would come some time, and we would take that train. Was it too much to ask that it might come soon?

'What are you reading?

'The autobiography of a famous war photographer.'

I knew he was reading that, of course. I had seen the book in his bag and had been waiting for him to start it.

'Can you read it aloud to me?'

'Are you sure you want me to?'

Am I sure I want him to, am I sure I want him to?

'Yes.'

He poured out more wine and took a sip before he began. I thought to myself that those were the last two sounds I would hear before he began reading from the killing fields to me, the sound of wine being poured into a glass and of him swallowing, and afterwards, when he had finished reading, maybe I would never hear anything more.

'"The Americans call photography an art. They have galleries, institutions, exhibitions. But what I'm doing is not art. How can I call it that? These pictures come from a witness. I've seen prisoners captured, stripped naked and blindfolded, trembling at the knees before someone gives the order to fire. I've seen men dragged out of cells at dawn and down to a market square before throngs of people, and a fire engine standing by to hose away the blood after the execution. I can't detach the image my camera produces from the images in my mind. I can't separate my photographs from their subjects. How can I talk of these photographs as art objects? These are real people. I have inhaled their suffering."'

There was the word: witness. If the train had arrived we could have climbed aboard and left the word lying on the table. We could have stood the wine carafe on it so that it didn't blow away, witness caught by the wind, police in search of witness. We could have stood at the train window, he behind me, watching the plastic table and its wine carafe and witness getting smaller and smaller until it had vanished completely and I could put my head out of the window into the wind and shout at it.

He laid the book down and pointed towards the horizon.

'The Falkland Islands are out there somewhere, aren't they?'

'If you say so, yes.'

'They're occupied by the British. And the British once established a philosophy they called empiricism.'

'Well?'

'Empiricism says that only that which can be observed is real. That which cannot be observed does not exist. That's why it's so important to have witnesses to the other reality, someone who can tell about it.'

'This is how the others die?'

'This is how the others die.'

'Even if people don't want to know about it?'

He didn't answer, simply picked up the book again and went on to read to me about the war photographer's astonishment at people's anger. Why should he have to defend himself? Did he create the reality he photographed? Was he responsible for the deaths of the people he photographed? Did he injure them, torture them, starve them? He was just a witness. If he hadn't taken the photographs, someone else would have, and if someone else hadn't, the public would have remained in comfortable ignorance of that reality. Was that what they actually wanted?

We waited in silence, and then he added, almost as an afterthought, 'I used to be a Gandhian. I believed in the doctrine that all living creatures are fundamentally one, and that violence against any living creature is thus violence against all; it doesn't matter *where* the violence occurs, the only thing that matters is *that* it occurs, and as a Gandhian there is only one thing you can do: seek out the violence and oppose it wherever it is taking place.'

'For instance by telling the world about it?'

'For instance.'

'And what are you now?'

'I don't know.'

Oh yes you do. You can see as well as I can that the doctrine is aimed in two directions, and it's typical of you to mention only one. The other is that violence against yourself is violence to others, and where does that leave you and me?

November 29th
Telephone call from home. Separatist movement in the north. Troops sent.

December 2nd
Ibrahim. Letter. Muslim brotherhood. Weapons training. Ibrahim. For God's sake.

December 3rd
'What does he say?'

He had been sitting for some time watching me staring at the letter from Ibrahim, had seen me running my fingers over the short words and sentences and muttering.

'Not much.'

'But something?'

'He's copying cassettes.'

'Your liberation movement did that too.'

'Of course. It's the only possible medium in a country where over half the population can't read. We learnt from the Iranians. The Ayatollah led the revolt without leaving his suburban Paris villa; all he needed was a microphone and a good transmitter or telephone and within a few hours his speeches had been copied on to cassettes in their thousands and sent to the mosques for distribution. He reached the whole population.'

'Your liberation movement did that too.'

'You've already said that. You don't need to repeat it.'

'But there's one thing I haven't said.'

He was out of his chair and over my side of the table before I could escape. He did that sometimes, and that's when I realized I had forgotten how strong he was. He took my arms and held them behind my back so that he was standing with his arms round me. He pulled me up from the chair and held me close and asked in a whisper why Ibrahim was doing weapons training if he was only copying cassettes, and I tried to break free but he was holding me tight and whispering in the other ear why was he doing weapons training if he was only copying cassettes, and I shook my head as if to shake off his question, no, no, no, but it was still there, in his arms, in his body. Was Ibrahim lying or was it because he risked having to defend himself against someone? He caught me as my knees gave way and I fell against him crying, 'Ibrahim would never lie to me.'

December 5th

We have been to see a house. A little brick house with a corrugated-iron roof and a herb garden. As I locked the door behind us, I had the feeling of locking the door on a life. I could see that he had noticed it.

December 12th

People here are not real. They have no history, they have no ties. They have a future, but that belongs to the place, not to them.

PEACE

'Comrade President, Comrade Party Secretary, friends – Welcome, on this the final day of our National Assembly meeting.'

She didn't look right on the rostrum: I thought she was too young, too strong and too alive for a rostrum; she seemed irked by the microphone, as if it were in her way, irked by the lectern, as if it were a hindrance. I smiled; I understood.

Her first words were lost in the buzz of conversation from about two hundred people, half of them seated in the straight ranks of chairs in the auditorium, the rest standing in the gallery above. The light streaming through the Gothic windows high in the walls of the conference hall fell obliquely on to the audience in the chairs and glinted on uniform buttons and decorations. They were mostly men in their late forties, the women among them were younger; the youth of the country were in the gallery, animated and playful.

'I had a friend once, the same age as myself. We came from the same village, the same island, the same mosque. We joined the same branch of the Party, went to the same meetings, put up the same posters. There was a sense of companionship between us that I later came to realize was more than just friendship.'

Those seated in the auditorium exchanged glances and smiles, some nodded. The young people in the gallery observed her more dispassionately, unsure of who she was.

She represented the age group that for them had always been held up as an ideal, those who had gone before and raised the flag.

'We signed up as volunteers together, took the same ferry to the mainland, travelled in the same bus across the country, rode in the same truck up into the mountains with other volunteers. I remember it so well, there were three trucks in convoy, full of young people, boys and girls, proud, eager, excited. We sang the Party songs we had learnt at meetings, and the battle songs we learnt from the leaders on the trucks. It was a wonderful day, with bright sunshine and a gentle breeze from the mountains. We were so happy at being involved in something at last, doing something. I remember standing on the back of the truck hanging on to the frame behind the cab, my friend at my side, her long dark hair flowing in the wind. I caught it and held it and she turned to look at me, looked at me and smiled. That is one of the moments I know I shall always carry with me; there are some moments like that, I think, in the lives of all of us.'

I glanced round at the young boy behind me and caught his eye, he responded immediately with a swift grin, a tiny flash of pride. She was good, she engaged the interest of both hall and gallery with her voice and presence, it was impossible to ignore her, and she had aroused a certain respect in the audience, many of whom were craning forward in their seats, attentive, anxious not to miss anything.

'Another such moment was when I found her killed a year later. She was lying on her stomach with one leg doubled under her and her long hair pinned up. Her fingers had stiffened round her rifle, her eyes were wide open and staring, as if in incomprehension. Comrade President, comrade Party Secretary, friends, I propose a minute's silence and a battle salute in memory of my friend and the fifty thousand young people who lost their lives in the war. Rolex was her *nom de guerre*. She was given it in the first camp we came to. I remember her being amused by it. Rolex is dead. Long live Rolex.'

I had to bite my lip. The youth behind me put his hand on my arm and squeezed gently. She had lowered her voice, almost whispering the last words that rippled over the audience and up into the gallery like rings on water, washing over faces and eyes and infusing them with solemnity. Hundreds of chairs scraped the floor as the audience rose and held their left hands clenched in the air in salute. The young people in the gallery straightened up and stood to attention, and the minute blended with the sunshine coming in through the windows and flooding the hall. The seconds ticked slowly towards eternity, as if we had stepped out of time and were standing in a cathedral of memories. My eyes were riveted on her as she stood with clenched fist and her gaze scanned the audience, and if the audience had not been so preoccupied with its own ritual, its own gratification, it might have sensed a warning sign, because her eyes were fiery. Instead the hall was caught totally off guard by the voice that suddenly burst into the minute, straight into the silence.

'I wonder whether my friend would have smiled if she had been standing where I am standing now and seen all the Rolexes. A room full of mature men, tall, elegant men, and every one with a Rolex. Some in silver, some in gold, some with inlaid jewels. In my village there is not a single Rolex, and half an hour's donkey ride from the village people don't even know what a Rolex is. But here, in this room, every one of the men has a Rolex.'

The murmur of a hundred voices welled up in protest, seeking mutual support. She cut right through it.

'Are they gifts? From foreign diplomats? Or companies? Are they bribes? From whom? And for what? Or were they bought honestly? In which case, where did the money come from?'

She was shouting, clipping each word so that it vibrated in the air over the dumbstruck audience. Then she suddenly dropped the volume, spoke in a soft and menacing voice.

'A Rolex is a status symbol even for Europeans. Our Party has always been poor: we couldn't afford modern weapons, we couldn't afford modern communications equipment, we couldn't afford modern field hospitals, we couldn't afford anything that might have saved the lives of any of the fifty thousand young people who died. But now suddenly everyone can afford a Rolex, a luxury.'

She flared her nostrils and jutted out her chin.

'Dior?'

She sniffed a little more.

'Armani?'

Two officers in the front row made a sign, and I heard rifles being moved on to shoulders behind me. The young boy put his arm in mine and held tight, and I could tell that he was doing the same with the man on the other side of him. I didn't know how many there were of them, of us, throughout the room. I felt a hand on my shoulder, someone trying to push me to one side, but I braced my legs and body and stood firm. The hand tried again, tried to push through between the boy and myself, but we stood firm.

'There's one thing I haven't said yet.'

She looked at me as she spoke, let her eyes dwell on me for a brief instant.

'My friend was shot in the back. She was one of those chosen as a personal aide to our commander. We all know what that means. But she went along with it, it was part of her sacrifice, we all made sacrifices to win this war. She knew something about him, something she threatened to tell if he didn't leave her alone, she had witnessed something. Now the witness is dead. Very convenient.'

A voice in the hall screeched out its anger, heads turned in astonishment. The guards behind us were rushing to and fro trying to find a way through.

'But I am here. And I stand here as a witness that the Party has stabbed all the other fifty thousand in the back. I have been in contact with what are called the separatists in the north. They are not separatists, that's a lie, they are peasants who have risen in protest against the land reform, a reform that takes away their lands and makes them over to industrial use. Did my friend and the other fifty thousand die so that we could set soldiers against peasants?'

The murmur in the gallery was growing into a roar, punctuated by louder cries.

'I have been in contact with the Muslim Brotherhood and seen their weapons. They are our old weapons, and believe me, I know what I'm talking about. The Brotherhood have not stolen the weapons, they've got them from people in this room. Did my friend and the other fifty thousand die so that we could arm religious fundamentalists?'

She was shouting at the top of her voice now, above the commotion from the gallery, above the angry outbursts and clenched fists in the hall, above the sound of the boots of the guards who had managed to get round and were racing towards the podium. Ibrahim leaned over my shoulder and took the tape I had extracted from the cassette player. I could feel his coolness, the freshness of his taut clean skin and his suppleness. He brushed my arm lightly, held the tape up momentarily for his sister to see from the rostrum, and disappeared. She smiled.

Late evening alone by the window with my notebook:
    'Did that happen or was it a dream? My dream of her?
    'What does it mean, that something is real? That it exists as an idea, or that it has form and content? The Platonic or the Aristotelian model of reality? Or is the real that which

endures? In either case dreams are real: they exist as ideas, her speech was an idea, but was it hers or mine? Dreams also have both form and content, because water can dream. And dreams endure, they pass down from generation to generation. If reality can be graded, and is not just an either/or, real/unreal, then dreams are more real than we are, because they continue, we are born into life and dream for a short while before we die, but dreams continue.'

It was raining. I looked out at the rain, felt a sense of loss at her absence and went on writing:

'Is it possible to convey reality? We are taught to believe so, to believe that it can be conveyed by language. What madness.'

I watched the rain a little longer, crossed out the last sentence and went on writing:

'Can God be conveyed? Should He be? We are influenced by natural science, which has persuaded us that the reality of physics can be conveyed by formulae; if only the language is precise enough, the reality of man can be conveyed just as exactly. That is wrong. Science can convey the laws of nature with its formulae, but cannot convey chance, nor the individual.'

I closed my notebook and thought that there was no law of nature in my missing her, the longing was my own. Then I started packing to travel to another dream, the last. I packed in the certain knowledge that something was over. I didn't know what it was, but I was in no doubt, something was over, and it was just a question of time before I understood what it was. First to Shangri-La, humanity's collective dream of the eternal idyll, described in the thirties by James Hilton in *Lost Horizon*, later filmed, and nowadays imprinted on our consciousness by boutiques and luxury hotels. The place exists: it's a mountain pass with a monastery in Tibet.

Shangri-La, the place where there is no conflict and people do not change: for human beings the germ of conflict lies in change; Shangri-La, the place where there is no violence and no disease and no ageing; Shangri-La, the place where all the things we fear most do not even exist as ideas, they have to be brought there, by us.

———

'What do you know about him?'

His editor was a handsome man, with long grey hair and large, steady hands. He downed espresso the way we drink tea, and stopped talking whenever a noisy vehicle drove past, as if he had all the time in the world.

'In our culture we ask fewer questions than you do.'

He pulled out a silver cigarette case from his inside pocket, opened it and proffered it to me. That was one of the things I liked about him: he must have been one of the last Europeans who had the time to take cigarettes out of the packet and transfer them neatly into a case; one of the last Europeans who would never think of lighting a cigarette if he were with a woman without offering one to her first, regardless of how many times she had declined.

'And he doesn't say anything? You don't ask, and he doesn't tell?'

'We have enough to talk about in the present.'

'Have you shown him your village?'

'Yes.'

'Has he shown you his village?'

'No.'

The editor tapped his cigarette against the lid of the cigarette case and smoothed it over his lips. That was another thing I liked about him: he had rituals. 'Always look for rituals in a man,' my mother used to say, 'that will give you the key to him. My men always fall off cliffs, and that makes me sure of them.'

'Perhaps he doesn't come from a village?'

'He does. But it no longer exists.'

That's what I can never manage to get used to with Europeans: they're capable of saying the oddest things.

'Has it struck you that he's obviously not Italian, yet he works as a reporter for an Italian paper?'

'Yes. But I don't know how far removed from one another your languages are.'

'Quite a lot.'

An open sports car accelerated past, and he paused, enough for me to feel a tension, as if I were facing something I wasn't sure I wanted to.

'His Italian is fluent, but that wasn't the reason we wanted him on the staff.'

My mother used to say there was one certain way to get men to stop talking, and I felt inclined to do it now, but there was no question of it; the editor was a practising Catholic and we were sitting in a European pavement café. European women don't do such things, not in pavement cafés, and certainly not with practising Catholics.

'He came here as a young man in search of something. He met some Jesuits and joined the Order. Do you know what they believe in?'

'He's told me about them.'

He had told me about them many times, but he had just never said anything about how involved he was with them.

'Does he still belong to them?'

'In a way.'

When I get hold of him, I think I shall start by slicing him into little pieces and then let him fry for a long time, in his own fat, while I beat him in the frying pan with the palm of my hand and scream.

'In what way?'

The editor smiled.

'He's still in contact with the Society. They know about you.'

'In what way does he belong to the Jesuits?'

'After he broke off his theology studies – that was where I first met him, I was his teacher – after he broke off his theology studies he went abroad, travelling with a Jesuit priest on an assignment. I don't know where, the Jesuits never say, but I think it was to the Third World.'

'Somebody has to be in third place, I suppose.'

'Sorry. I didn't mean it like that.'

He sat in silent contemplation of the table for a moment. That's an enchanting trait in Catholics, instant atonement.

'Three years later he came back a changed man. Nothing dramatic, but much quieter.'

'And?'

'And there was a distance that hadn't been there before. As if he was standing back and observing us.'

'How did he come to this paper?'

'We were looking for a reporter. The Jesuits recommended him. He fitted perfectly.'

'Just a general reporter?'

'A rather special reporter.'

So it was you; he came back changed, and you just turned him round and sent him out again. Shall I tell you something about that quietness, about that distance? First you would have to hear his laughter, feel his closeness, and then just switch it off, click, and out, suddenly you're sitting alone beneath a grey sky on a grey plain, with no warning, you don't know how long you'll have to sit there or how you came to be there, and above all, my friend, my silver-haired friend in the black suit and the white collar, above all you don't know what you have to do to get away from there, you can shout and scream and strike out, but it doesn't help: your screams turn into grey flowers and your blows into grey birds, you can weep and beg and plead, but it doesn't help: your tears turn into grey water and your prayers into grey wind. And now I know something I didn't know before: he didn't seek this out on his own, he had help.

'It seems as if the Jesuits accept responsibility for what happened, they're protecting him.'

'Are they really? Where can I find the priest he travelled with?'

'I'm not at liberty to say.'

'Is that so?'

I leaned back. My mother used to say if you get angry and it's not a suitable time to show it, lean back and move your body, that will take your mind off it.

'What are you doing?'

'Just moving.'

'Good God, we're sitting in a café.'

'Oh yes, so we are.'

The editor tried to look as if he didn't know me, but failed; as if he were sitting at a separate table, but failed. In the end he gave up and turned to face me again.

'Can you please stop that?'

'Where will I find him?

He wrote down an address on a piece of paper.

'Don't say who gave it to you. I'll get you a letter of introduction from his superior.'

'Do you know where he is now?'

'In Tibet. May I ask you something?'

'What about?'

'I want to ask you about his work. He has always covered wars for us. We have asked him to cover dreams. He was not happy about it, and he does it his way, but he does it, and not only because I asked him to. Why?'

'Don't you know?'

'I want to hear it from you.'

'He travels to these dreams because some people need them, some long for them.'

'Who?'

'He needs them.'

'Just him?'

'I long for them.'

'Have you both lost your dreams?'

'Or forsaken them.'

'How?'

'In what way, how?'

'I don't know.'

'Nor do I.'

But that isn't true, I think to myself. I know both how people lose their dreams in a war and how they forsake them, and if you want to know anything about that, you can come to our place when we're in bed and afraid to sleep, because sleep means nightmares, bloody nightmares that never end, and if you want to know more about that, you can come to our place when we're standing watching the rain, we can stand at the window for hour upon hour watching the rain, and neither of us says 'I wish it would stop raining', because that sentence would express a wish for something different, and by extension that could mean wishing I were someone different, and that is the sentence that weaves dreams: I wish I were a different person, I wish I had children, riches, power, I wish I could start afresh. It is that ability that violence deprives you of, the ability to wish you were someone else. Violence changes a person, not only the one who is a victim of violence, but also the one who perpetrates it or witnesses it, you lose the ability to see yourself holding a child with the hands you have used to kill, you lose the ability to see people in white dancing towards you with the eyes that have seen mutilations, and if you think you can hear an echo of him in this, it is because these sentences are said in the middle of the night, either by him or by me.

I looked at the editor.

'Is there anything else you want to know?'

'His writing. His style is changing. If I imagine him within a circle, he seems to be writing more and more towards the periphery, away from the centre.'

'How?'

'He went off to write about a massacre, the people from the north against the people from the south, different ethnic backgrounds, different religions. His news reports are always straightforward; who, what, where, when and, if possible, why; past tense, no first-person narrator, not interposing himself between the reader and the news. When he writes feature articles, he usually goes over to the present and writes himself into the story – that's as close as any reporter can get.'

'But this time?'

'Third person, past tense. For him that's the equivalent of taking a step back. It must have been quite something for him to have had to do that. That worries me. But there's something else that worries me more.'

'What?'

'He's slipping over into fiction.'

The editor rummaged in his briefcase, pulled out a folded newspaper, opened it, and looked at me:

'Tension is mounting in the region. The people from the south have been attacked inside their churches and in their houses. A thousand of them have sought refuge in the police station, and are then taken under escort to the railway station. A train has come to evacuate them, six steel container wagons, and two open wagons. Loading has been completed, the wagons are crammed full, and five hundred people from the south are waiting in an area the police have cordoned off at the side of the station. The reporter, 'he', is standing on the platform when the mob from the north arrives. I'll just read the end:

' "Three young boys came first, rolling a barrel of diesel oil in front of them, gently, gracefully. Behind them a kaleidoscope of colours, like a billowing landscape, coming nearer and nearer. He shut his eyes and listened, listened to the drums, the singing, the cries, nearer and nearer. Then he opened his eyes and saw the mob surge into the station, pouring in over the whole station area and meeting resistance, which always releases more strength.

' "From a little way off music could be heard, it sounded like a concerto; he shaded his eyes and saw a man sitting playing a cello beneath a tree at the edge of a clearing, a cool breeze ruffling the sheet music on its music stand. Mozart: logical, predictable; the concerto was one written for piano, but he was pleased the man was playing the melody on the cello, without the left-hand's bass accompaniment; it sounded softer like that, more coherent, the notes flowing into one another. He added the bass himself, humming under his breath, turned round and saw a woman being pulled down from the nearest goods wagon and opened with a machete from throat to belly, and then a man in a red cap hacked off one of her arms and held it up like a trophy. He went on humming the accompaniment as firewood was stacked under the six container wagons, splashed with diesel oil and set alight; he went on humming as the first burning mattresses were thrown into the enclosure of five hundred people. The cello had reverted to the theme now, but more strongly, more extensively, as if the cellist had become more confident; he could develop the bass accompaniment more.

' "Slowly and carefully he tore the pages out of his notebook, one by one, screwed them up and set fire to them. Then he picked up two stones and smashed his camera with calm, measured blows till all that remained were fragments of glass and pieces of metal. He scraped red earth with his hands and feet until the fragments of glass and the pieces of metal were covered, then he stood up and walked off, away from the station precinct, away from the smell of burnt flesh in the container wagons, away from the screams in the burning enclosure." '

I stopped the editor's reading.

'Fast forward. I know what burnt flesh smells like.'

He cast his eyes down the page, glanced up at me.

'The reporter goes through the town, through an inferno, corpses at every crossroads and in every doorway. At the hospital, fifty women from the north are blocking the entrance, beating back all those from the south; a bleeding old man carried by two others, a woman with a lifeless child in her arms. Beyond the doors he can hear patients begging for their lives. Let me read you the last few lines:

' "He went on until he found what he was looking for, a teenage girl impaled on a stake, thick where it entered her vagina, thinner where it protruded from her mouth. The stake had straightened her neck and pressed her head back, as if she was looking up at the heavens. The remains of her clothes were hanging from her arms and over her right foot. The blood on the stake was congealed and black, there was the sweet smell of putrefaction, vultures had pecked holes in her left side. The girl looked down at him.

'What are you doing here?'

'Exploring the darkness.'

'Why?'

'I don't know.'

Only when I had watched the editor disappear out of sight down the street, only when I was standing alone in the carriage of an underground train with my knuckles pressed to my lips to stop myself screaming out loud, only then did I whisper to myself that his writing is changing because he is on the verge of leaving reality. When he reaches the circumference, he'll carry on out of the circle altogether.

Rome, Rome and the smell of steps, so different from back home. One set of steps is Spanish, the others are Italian, so sweet, come on, let's build some Spanish steps here; the smell of Spanish, of Italian, and the sound of my footsteps in an alley, I could hear they were nervous, *insha'Allah*, and my breath, my breath, *insha'Allah*. A heavy door with a brass plate: *Institutum Historicum Societatis Iesu*. I ran my fingers over the letters, said them one by one, *Institutum Historicum Societatis Iesu*, turned to see whether there was anyone I could ask, a young man, with long hair and a guitar case, his arm very thin and cold to my touch, the Jesuits' Historical Institute, he said, smiling and walking on. Still mesmerized by the brass plate, I only just remembered to call out my thanks. I had the same feeling as on night patrol during the war, the same feeling of danger, the same feeling of uncertainty, who is doing the hunting and who is being hunted? I opened the gate, a courtyard, a door, and more steps down into the darkness.

'How did you find me?'

The Jesuit priest did not look up to see who it was, nor did the light from the naked bulb above him, it continued to shine down on the bowed head and the black robe as if afraid of losing him.

'A friend told me the way.'

'Remarkable.'

He didn't look up even as he spoke, just carried on perusing the sheet of paper he was holding. I went over to him with the letter his superior had written and he put down what he was engaged on and took it, read its three sentences and nodded. Then he folded it and placed it on top of a pile of letters, changed his mind and put it on top of another pile, changed his mind again and put it on top of a third, then picked it up and read it again, as if uncertain. I counted.

'There are fifteen piles of letters on that desk. If you carry on like this we'll be well into next week before you get round to asking me why I'm here.'

'You're quite right.'

He took off his spectacles and turned to face me. I gasped.

'Yes, I know. People have always said how alike we looked. But especially after we came back.'

It was the expression. Not the same eyes, not the same complexion, but the same expression. He pulled up a chair for me.

'What can I do for you?'

'Tell me what happened.'

He was the same age, slim, fit, still retaining the physique of a life in the field.

'Can I offer you a cup of coffee?'

His voice had an oddly tremulous quality, as if it were little used, or under pressure.

'No thanks. Just tell me what happened.'

He looked at me long and hard before rising to his feet.

'You will have a cup of coffee.'

He went over to a bureau with a hotplate on it, took an espresso pot out of a drawer, filled it with water from a mug, switched on; coffee, cups, sugar: I could see from his movements that they were not a way of playing for time, they were a journey back into the past. I inspected the room: a whitewashed cellar, a small window with a grille high up on one wall, the door I had come in by, a closed door on the opposite wall, the desk with its letters, the bureau, our two chairs and the bulb in the ceiling.

'I've been expecting you.'

He brought the cups over, gave me one, placed his own on his chair. He was squinting, fumbling, as if he had poor vision.

'Has he told you about me?'

'We don't meet any more. The others have spoken of you.'

'Why don't you meet?'

'If you wait a while, you'll understand.'

He turned off the hotplate and picked up the pot, fumbling slightly for the switch and the handle, then came and sat down, poured out the coffee laboriously, remembered the sugar, got up, put his cup back on the chair, crossed over to the bureau. Watching him, I whispered *insha'Allah* to myself, must I do this, dare I do this, when an established priest with years of field experience is so unwilling to go into it?

'I rather want to tell you first what I'm working on here.'

He inclined his head towards the desk as he said it, holding his cup and saucer in both hands, taking a sip.

'In this cellar we have stored all the letters from brothers serving in the field since the Order was founded in 1456. That's something in excess of eighteen thousand letters. I'm cataloguing them for the archive.'

'Are you saying that the Order hasn't had them catalogued before?'

'Yes, they have, but only by name and year. Name of sender and recipient.'

'And you?'

'By subject. I'm reading all the letters and cataloguing them by subject.'

'What kind of subjects?'

'Baptism, redemption, healing, revelation, communion, things like that.'

Things like that. The priest was in another world now and I froze: I knew that what was coming next would come from there.

'They hacked them into little pieces. First they hacked off whatever could be hacked off, arms, legs, genitals, ears, noses, and the victims were still alive, then they hacked out parts of the body itself, and still the victims were alive, still they screamed.'

He closed his eyes and screamed himself, a long-drawn-out despairing sobbing scream, like a heart pumping blood out of a body that is hacked apart. The bulb above the desk swayed in agitation, looking down on him.

'We were sitting eating our evening meal when the massacre started. A boy came running in to tell us, frightened out of his wits. The massacre had been brewing up for days, the radio had been hammering the message home, *crush the cockroaches, crush the cockroaches*, but we were hoping against hope to the end. He had asked the priest in the local church to prepare to take in refugees, to have food, water and blankets ready so that people could seek sanctuary in the church until the worst of the frenzy was over. As soon as the boy had spoken we got on our bicycles and went round the areas we knew were most at risk, banging on doors and getting people to gather in the church. Several times we passed bands of murderers and were hardly able to believe they would let us alone. Your friend was the first to get back. The local priest had locked the refugees into the church and given the keys to the murderers. They had gone in with machetes. All were dead except for a boy on his knees at the altar, the one who had brought us the warning; he had his arms wrapped around himself as if to hold himself upright. Your friend went down on his knees at the boy's side and took his hands to pray with him; the boy's intestines slid out of the long machete cut he had been holding together. Your friend sat with the boy in his arms until he died. Has he not told you about all this?'

'He's told me some of it. We talk about war as little as possible. I haven't told him about all the times I have killed, and he hasn't told me about all the times he has seen someone killed. We have given enough of our life to war as it is. What happened to the local priest?'

'He was protected.'

'By whom?'

'By the Church. By us.'

The priest made an arc with his arm, as if to take in the whole of Rome, or at least the Vatican. Then he looked at me:

'Your friend has been back there eight times, right? Every time he returns with new names. Every time he goes to see our superiors and shows them his material, tells them that it is there for everyone to find, asks them if the Church prefers to be ahead of disclosures or behind. In his usual mild manner.'

'I know what you mean.'

'If he could choose, I think he would keep going back until every faithless servant had been weeded out.'

'What happened to you two?'

A long pause.

'We each went our own way. He's out there now. I sit here cataloguing God's love.'

'Was that just chance, or was it something you agreed on?'

Pause. Then he stood up and took my cup, gestured to his eyes.

'My sight is failing, I'm running out of time. So is he.'

Insha'Allah, insha'Allah. The sound of my footsteps going down Spanish and Italian steps and into an alley, the same alley, through a gate, the same gate, but six months later. This time he was having to hold what he was reading very close to his eyes: spectacles and light bulb in one hand and letter in the other. He was using the spectacles as a magnifying glass and holding the light bulb right up to the paper.

'Do you know where he is?'

'Yes.'

He turned towards me and I lowered my gaze. I couldn't

bear to see his expression, not now. He drew up a chair for
me.

'Coffee?'

I nodded.

He brought out cups, the same cups, the same tentative
fumbling movements, only more so. It seemed as if he had an
idea where the cups were and was groping for them without
seeing them, the bulb above the desk following his actions
with sadness. He was thinner, weaker.

'Tell me about God.'

He couldn't manage to get the top off the espresso
pot, lifted a corner of his robe and tried to grip it with
that. Sandal, grey sock, bare leg, it made him look
vulnerable.

'I have no God.'

I took the espresso pot from him and loosened the top. He
thanked me a little uncertainly.

'The one you used to have.'

'The Merciful, the Gracious, the Holy, the Creator, the
Forgiving, the All-Knowing, the All-Seeing, the All-Hearing,
the Judge, the Giver of Life, the Giver of Death, the Manifest,
the Hidden, the Avenger, the Equitable, the Guide to the
Right Path. Shall I go on?'

'Exactly. God's ninety-nine names. Has your father got a
string of ninety-nine beads, one for each name?'

'Had. I inherited it.'

'Where is it?'

'In my pocket.'

'Always?'

'Yes.'

He looked directly at me. I met his gaze, and for the first
time I could see the difference between them, for the first time
I could see why the one went off and the other stayed. I held
his gaze, stopped him in what he had intended saying.

Something cold entered the room. He gave me a cup, fetched his own and sat down.

'Have you read anything about cognition theory?'

'We didn't have much time for that during the war.'

'I'm sorry.'

'That's OK.'

He took a sip of coffee while he atoned. Then he looked at me again.

'For you Muslims God is concrete, he has ninety-nine names, one for every quality. For us Christians God is abstract, so that knowing anything at all about Him is a problem.'

'I'm not a Muslim.'

'Sorry.'

He took another sip of atonement.

'Look at the paradox: we believe in a God that we don't know whether we can know anything of. Broadly speaking there are three views. God by His Grace lets us know what we need to know about Him.'

He stirred his coffee.

'Or we read our desires into God and create an image of Him for ourselves that way, without ever getting to know anything about Him. All we know about is our own sense of longing.'

He raised his head and looked up at the little window high in the wall.

'Or we get to know something about God just by letting ourselves merge into Him, like the Mystics. You people have it in Sufism, we have it in Spinozism.'

'I'm not a Muslim.'

'Sorry.'

He removed his spectacles and rubbed the bridge of his nose. He seemed tired.

'You can find a parallel in secular cognition theory. It has, also broadly speaking, three models of the relationship between the perceiving subject and the object perceived. In the first the object yields knowledge to the subject, in the second the subject reads the knowledge it wants into the object, in the third the subject acquires knowledge by letting itself merge with the object.'

'Can you demonstrate with an image?'

'Image?'

He looked at me quizzically.

'An image I can see in front of me and understand, of a traveller, for example. A traveller is either influenced by the reality he is studying, or finds the reality he wants to find, or has to let himself merge with the reality he is studying in order to find out about it. Is that it?'

'I can hear him in your words. Has he said more?'

'No.'

'Typical.'

'What more is there to say?'

'Are you familiar with the problem of evil?'

'He's talked to me about it.'

'And what has he said?'

'If God is love, why does it not show? And if God is almighty, why does He rule the world in so miserable a manner?'

'Right, his words, but right nevertheless. That's the biggest problem for Christianity, and a very embarrassing one. The commonest answer is that evil exists because God created man with free will.'

'He calls that a superficial answer.'

'I know. It leads directly to a further question: Where does mankind get its evil from? Is there an evil power in the world, opposed to the power of God? The Christian Church is divided on the issue, and there are as many answers as there are creeds.'

'What's your answer?'

'John, chapter 9, verse 3: Jesus met a man who was born blind, and his disciples asked him who had sinned, his parents or the man himself, since he was born blind? Jesus answered that neither had, he had been born blind so that God's love could be made manifest in him. Then Jesus spat on the ground and made a paste with which he anointed the man's eyes so that he could see.'

'Jesus.'

'You may well say that. So in your friend's case I think it's a matter of recording God's absence, so that God's love can be made manifest. I think it also has something to do with the influence of Gandhi on him; as long as violence exists it is your duty to seek it out and oppose it. And ultimately I think it's his way of being close to God, perhaps his most honest answer to the problem of evil, is Psalm 73, verse 28: "But it is good for me to draw near unto God: I have made the Lord God my refuge, That I may tell of all thy works." Joy in pain, hope in hopelessness.'

I could hear him whispering inside me now, uttering a warning, don't put it into words, don't put words to a process, because you'll capture it, trap it. But it was too late, the words were coming, spilling out.

'Is that what you are engaged on? Are you God's witnesses? Are you sitting here as witness to the good, while he's out travelling as witness to evil?'

I cried out the last words with tears in my voice. He put a hand on my arm.

'It's more complicated than that. But I don't think that's what you came to ask about.'

'What have I come to ask about, then?'

'Whereabouts in the process he is.'

'Do you know?'

'I think he began by recording evil, just as I record the good.'

'Why would that be necessary?'

'What else should we do with God's love?'

'And now?'

'Now I think he is on the point of merging with it. It's his strange and paradoxical atonement for the massacre we contributed to. Psalm 51, verses 16 to 17: "For thou desirest not sacrifice; else would I give it: thou delightest not in burnt offering. The sacrifices of God are a broken spirit: a broken and a contrite heart, O God, thou wilt not despise."'

A brown envelope with Italian stamps, like hearing him walk up the stairs, or put his key in the lock; a brown envelope with Italian stamps, and my hands pressed to my lips, just for a moment.

Did I go back home to open the letter or was I going home anyway? Did I sit on the bus for two nights and a day with the envelope on the seat by my side because I didn't dare open it, didn't dare expose my dreams to anything, or did I just want to wait until I was on the top of the island and could see him clearly?

I looked about me and smiled at the thought of what he would have noted: reggae music from the loudspeaker, of course; a car we passed with goats tied on the roof; the smell of the rose water that the woman in front bathed her face with every quarter of an hour; and he would have noted the time until he was quite sure that it was at quarter-hourly intervals; he would have noted the rain coursing between the paving stones down the hill to the harbour, and the unusual silence on the ferry, as if people were not quite sure they were doing the right thing.

He would have stopped taking notes when we berthed and would have just walked up the hill with me to my mother's house. I chatted to him the whole way and answered for him, I held out three fingers and pretended

I was holding his hand, I greeted neighbours and friends and nodded at him, as if to show him off, and they smiled and nodded back. I put down my rucksack at the gate of my mother's house and went on, past the school where I now teach, towards the steps that my father and his brothers had cut for me. I wanted to read first, then talk. I stopped at the first step and looked at it, looked at the love that was carved into it, listened to the strength in the hammer blows. I placed my foot on the step and felt his arms around me: standing at the kitchen unit preparing a meal and him coming up behind me and hugging me, wordlessly. I placed my foot on the next step and heard his voice: sitting together in the evening, his voice in the room as he tells me stories and makes me laugh, or asks me how I am and waits for my reply, or reads to me, or is upset by something, something out there. I placed my foot on another step and saw his eyes, those two mirrors that are never empty, that always have something to say, about joy, tenderness, despair. I climbed further on up the steps with his arms around me and his voice and his expression inside me, I turned and looked down on the houses, smaller with each step, almost unreal, as if they no longer had anything to do with me, as if they belonged to another world. I climbed the last few steps to the top of the cliff and saw his smile. Whenever we had been together and I had to leave, he used to stand and follow me with his eyes, and I could turn round after ten metres, fifty metres or a hundred metres and he would still be there smiling at me, and in that smile lay the whole of my being, the whole of my future, and the envelope with the Italian stamps called out, that's where you slipped up, my friend, that's where you slipped up, and I stood at the top of the cliff and looked out and said, yes, that's where I slipped up. Arms and voice and expression I could manage, but when it came to the smile, I slipped up. I sat on the ground and opened the envelope, separated the accom-

239

run till you feel a rush inside you, a sudden current, the rush of reincarnation, from rush you have come, to rush you shall go. I lean forward to shade him from the sun and he looks up in terror and sees me, runs with his eyes fixed on me, stumbles, falls. I help him up carefully with my pencil, insert the point under his right arm and lift him up, nudge him forward with the blunt end. He cries out as he runs, 'You were one of us once, why are you doing this?'

Run, monk, run, out of my life. One of you? Never a Tibetan, never a monk, but one of you? I take my eyes off him and examine the wild landscape, the steep slopes and the vertical mountainsides, the monastery of brown brick with four towers and a hipped dragon roof projecting above its walls, prayer flags flapping in the wind; I breathe in the thin air with its scent of bonfires and beans hung out to dry; I close my eyes and feel the old monk's arms around me, the one who took me in and made me one of them. He put his forehead against mine and held it there for a long time, half an hour, an hour. Something flowed from him and into me, from him and into me, a strength, a rush, Kalu Rinpoche reincarnated through thirteen generations, or the sense of community that all religion provides? When he let me go, he had something in his expression that I spent years trying to understand and put into words. I could see it as he slowly tied a band of protective energy round my neck; I could feel it when he later initiated me into the art of breathing meditation with a visualized light. Being one of them was something more than belonging to a community.

Run, monk, run, out of my life. Shangri-La is behind you now, and thus exists no more. It is a state of being, not a place, and when you leave a state of being that you are part of yourself, you change it. Shangri-La, the name of humanity's collective daydream, the state where only good exists, and no evil, the state where people do not age, for that is natural and therefore evil, the state where people never die, for that is natural and therefore evil.

'It was James Hilton who thought up that.'

'Watch where you're going.'

He is approaching the edge of the wood. I am looking at what awaits him on the other side of the wood, much nearer now. The soldiers have reached the top of the hill behind him, but have not got any closer, their calls are sounding fainter, their shots more unreal.

There is snow in the air, the flakes settling on the monk's brow and melting, mingling with his sweat and trickling down into his eyes and blinding him. I see him wiping his eyes every few metres. He is panting heavily, he's out of condition, weakened by the ascetic life, by religious self-absorption.

'You were one of us once. Why do you use such words?'

'Because they're appropriate. How many Chinese have your prayer flags halted? How many Tibetan girls has the incense protected? How many schools have you managed to keep open with the aid of meditation?'

'What would you have done?'

He is shouting in anger, fear and frustration.

'You've no right to ask me that, it's not my country.'

I poke him in the back with the point of my pencil as I reply, knock him over and drag him along the path. He is kicking and struggling.

'In Lhasa rebellion is smouldering beneath the surface; it only needs a spark to ignite it. The streets will explode with people in a matter of seconds, but they have to know that they have you leading them, it's you they look up to, can't you see that?'

'Violence is not an option for us.'

'Violence is an option for everybody!'

Now I'm the one who's shouting. I hurl the pencil into the path in front of him, he runs into it, puts his hand up to his head, runs on. I turn to look at the Chinese soldiers; two of them have dropped to the ground and are setting up a machine gun on a tripod; there will soon be an end to the monk, no more monk. I raise my pencil and write across the pale-blue sky, 'The Chinese can slaughter the first thousand, the first ten thousand, the first hundred thousand, but they cannot slaughter the whole Tibetan people. The world will intervene and bring it to an end.'

He stops to read it, stops on the path with his pursuers at his heels and his brown eyes glistening with sweat and melted snow, stops on the path and reads and smiles and speaks.

'If you believed that I would call you touchingly naive. But you don't even believe it yourself, you're just writing it. You know as well as I do that the Chinese can slaughter us to the last person without the world lifting a finger. China is the big new investment market for Western capital, a billion consumers and a growing middle class with purchasing power. Not a finger.'

He runs on, I call after him.

'Fifteen years ago you were in the majority, eighty to eighty-five per cent. Now you're down to fifty per cent, with the same number of Chinese. In fifteen years' time you'll be in the minority, a minority in your own country. The Tibetan language will die out, Tibetan culture will die out, and you just sit and watch. That's self-annihilation.'

'We don't cut down trees.'

'Don't give me that!'

I can hear my voice rising to a falsetto, out of control, and close my eyes to collect myself. I know he's right, Tibetans don't cut down living trees, they gather the wood they need from what has fallen, what nature gives. These are the people who once taught me that all living beings deep down are one, and that violence against any living creature is violence against all others.

'How do you defend the fact that monks starve themselves to death on hunger strike, or set themselves on fire in protest against Chinese policies?'

'We don't defend it.'

'Gandhi talked of what he called the non-violence of cowardice. Do you recognize yourself?'

'We're not Gandhians. Nor are you any longer, I suspect.'

He has reached the wood now. If the Tibetans had felled trees he would have seen what was awaiting him on the other side. Now all he sees are tree trunks and the dark shadows between them that admit him and the moss that receives him and softens his footfalls. I turn my attention to the Chinese soldiers: they are looking unsure of themselves. The two with the machine gun open fire, raking the wood with bullets from left to right and back again; then they pause and wait.

Bare feet, bare feet, bare feet running. I can see the monk in amongst the trees, still running, but more calmly now, as if aware of the soldiers' uncertainty. I stick my pencil in here and there and block his way, but he runs round it every time, without saying a word. He is coming to the end of the trees and to what lies beyond them, almost expectantly. He seems to notice something, sense something, detect something. He raises his head and looks towards the edge of the wood, slows down and finally comes to a complete halt by the final tree.

'No. This is something you've invented.'

'This is how it is.'

We peer at the horde of young people, the black headbands, the rasta braids, the uniforms. They are all in their twenties, all armed, with spears, bows and arrows, long knives. Some of them have painted white streaks on their cheeks, vertical white streaks. There are only two women in the group, and they are athletic, self-assured, born leaders.

'You've seen this in country after country and so you've transposed it to us. But it's not like that here.'

'It's like that everywhere. It's just you who don't want to see it. Violence is a natural human mode of expression, it provides a sense of identity and appeals most strongly to those with the greatest need to express themselves.'

I let my pencil glide over the crowd of young people as I talk, let it bounce from head to head, and the youths look up with a smile, make a grab for it. I open the neck of one of the young women's blouses with the point of the pencil and she brushes it away with a laugh and does up her button again.

'Don't you understand that you are denying something archetypal when you deny violence? Violence is part of the human being, like sexuality, and laughter, and play. It comes of its own accord, as a natural reaction, exactly like sexuality and laughter and play. A younger generation will take repression for so long and no longer before turning to violence.'

I write *Patriotic re-education of all teachers* in the air above the head of the other young woman, and she snatches the sentence and holds it up like a banner; the youths in headbands and rasta braids shout out and clench their fists. I write *Parents in prison* and the crowd

245

shouts louder; I write *Chinese as official language* and *Chinese monopoly of the labour market* and the young people scream in rage, banging their weapons together. The two young women hold up a flag and start walking, fast, the flag billowing out above and behind them, and the rest of the young people follow them at a run. They are all shouting now, some are singing, the two young women, laughing at the top of their voices, strike up a slogan and get a response from behind. I look at the monk.

'See how stylish they are. How graceful. Something happens to the human body when it lives out its primeval instincts. It's as if it composes itself, finds both centre of gravity and sense of direction.'

The monk does not reply.

I opened the accompanying letter and put my hand over what was written there, put my hand over what was written there and closed my eyes. I could hear the sea better with my eyes closed, feel the warmth of the sun better. Just sit still for a moment, a brief moment, and let my heart settle down. Then I opened my eyes carefully and looked at the first line: it was my name; and I could hear him on the steps below me, he was singing, and a bird took his song and flew out with it over the sea. I moved my hand and looked at the next line, the first word: 'We'. I called it out, yes, that's us, you and me, and I heard him laugh, laugh and shout yes, yes, yes, and the breeze off the sea took his laughter and spread it over the island, and the whole island laughed, rang with laughter, and people looked up and smiled. I moved my hand further and read the whole line: 'We have not heard from him for six months.' Of course you haven't, nor have I, but what does it matter, he's here now.

I went over to the top step and looked down, step by step,

one at a time, wanting to make the dream last. The wind was still, no birds, no sounds, nothing, the steps were empty, and as the letter began its flight to the sea below I saw a man far, far away stand up from a desk full of letters and extinguish a naked light bulb hanging from the ceiling.

A NOTE ON THE TYPE

The text of this book is set in Bembo, the original types for which were cut by Francesco Griffo for the Venetian printer Aldus Manutius, and were first used in 1495 for Cardinal Bembo's *De Aetna*. Claude Garamond (1480–1561) used Bembo as a model and so it became the forerunner of standard European type for the following two centuries. Its modern form was designed, following the original, for Monotype in 1929 and is widely in use today.